Belated Follower

Also by Colleen L. Reece
in Large Print:

Alpine Meadows Nurse
Everlasting Melody
The Heritage of Nurse O'Hara
In Search of Twilight
Nurse Julie's Sacrifice

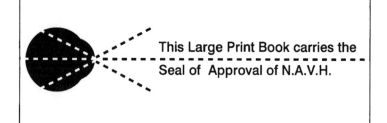

Belated Follower

Colleen L. Reece

Thorndike Press • Thorndike, Maine

Thorndike Press Large Print Christian Fiction Series.

The text of this Large Print edition is unabridged.
Other aspects of the book may vary from the original edition.

Set in 16 pt. Plantin by PerfecType.

Library of Congress Cataloging-in-Publication Data

Reece, Colleen L.
  Belated follower / Colleen L. Reece.
    p. cm.
  ISBN 0-7862-2861-X (lg. print : hc : alk. paper)
    1. Shepherds in the Bible — Fiction. 2. Bible. N.T. —
History of Biblical events — Fiction. 3. Jesus Christ —
Fiction. 4. Large type books. I. Title.
PS3568.E3646 B45 2000
 813'.54—dc21   00-059960

Belated Follower

Part 1

one

Purple dusk crouched low over the Judaean hills. A small fire stretched yellow fingers of light into surrounding shadows and rested on a bleating lamb searching for his mother. A joyful "baaa" rang out when he found her and settled with the rest of the flock.

Two men stood silhouetted against the encroaching, indigo night — youth and age, bearing unmistakable traces of kinship in their height, olive skin, and far-seeing dark eyes, trained to spot danger for the flock. Ara, the white-haired shepherd, exuded inner strength to match the meaning of his name — lion. Hard years had bent his back but not his magnificent spirit.

"It is well, Benjamin, son of my right hand. Come, let us prepare our meal."

The stripling lad hastened to help his father, pride swelling within him. Was not Ara leader of the shepherds, the one who sought heedless lambs and strayed sheep? Did not their friends call on his gentle touch to tend wounds from sharp stones and cruel thorns? Those same tender, calloused hands sometimes rested on Benjamin's head in blessing.

"You are a comfort in my old age, my son." As so often happened, the special bond between the two formed because Benjamin's mother had died in birthing him. "I waited so long for a child — a son. Long after hope flickered low, God sent you." Ara's white locks gleamed in the firelight and his eyes grew soft. "If your mother could see you now, she, too, would be proud."

"No boy — man — could ask for a better father," Benjamin replied. When they sat for their simple meal and Ara pronounced a blessing on the food, his son stored each moment in his heart. One day, perhaps soon, the lion would die. Yet the wealth of shared experiences could never die, only become rich treasures.

The sheep lay quietly under an inverted bowl of stars. Shepherds from neighboring flocks came and huddled around the merry fire. Benjamin sat silently, as befitted the youngest shepherd. His heartbeat quickened. Ears made keen by the cries of animals in distress missed no word of the older men's talk. His gaze turned to Ara. How tired he looked! Did the deceptively strong body conceal a hidden sickness? The night had not turned cold, yet his father trembled as if touched by the cold winds that blew in winter.

"Too tired to make merry with us?" their good friend Abner inquired.

Benjamin sprang to his feet. "My father never tires." His eyes flashed in the firelight. "This day I watched him chase a wolf from the flock. The beast fled before the might of Ara's rod."

Abner raised a shaggy eyebrow in surprise. "I meant no disrespect."

Ara glanced from shepherd to shepherd. "My son is quick to defend me, but there is no need." His smile changed the furrowed face to youth once more. "I have been thinking about the Messiah."

Benjamin caught his breath and sank back to the ground. The Messiah. Even the name had power to still jesting and cause the men to stare at Ara. To simple, hard-working men who kept their flocks, the promise of a deliverer beckoned more clearly than knowing the sun would rise in the east on the morrow.

"Father, tell us of the Messiah," Benjamin pleaded.

"I have told you many times, my son."

"Yea. Yet this night is so beautiful, so . . ." He spread wide his arms to the night sky now spattered with light from countless stars. "We have waited so long. Will the Messiah come soon?"

"He must if I am to see Him." Pain contorted Ara's features and his gnarled hands worked. "I long to see Him, then I can rest in peace."

"As do we all." Abner — rough, rude, yet whose name meant light — sighed and hunched forward. In the dim firelight his face softened with feelings he kept hidden during the daylight hours. Then, throwing caution to the night winds that sang softly in the distance, he raised his head and asked the question Benjamin knew troubled them all. "When the Messiah comes, what will He have to do with such as us? He is to be of royal birth, of the House of David. How can poor shepherds of the field hope to see such a One?"

Sternness wiped clean the longing in Ara's face. "Abner, have you forgotten the sacred writings?" His voice rolled out like a prophet of old destined to warn the people of the earth of that to come. "Did not Isaiah tell us He will be a deliverer; that the government will be on His shoulder? He shall be called wonderful, counselor, the mighty God, the everlasting Father, the Prince of Peace." Ara rose to full height, towering over the others. "Does not your heart burn within you at those words? What of Isaiah's further words, 'of the increase of His government and peace there shall be no end; upon the throne of David, and upon His kingdom, to order it and to establish it with judgment and justice from henceforth even forever.' The zeal of the Lord of hosts will perform this!"

Benjamin's heart stirred at the words his father had taught him from the time he could first understand. The promises of God rang in the night and echoed from the hills.

Abner looked ashamed at his doubts, yet other faces reflected them when he cried from the depths of a fearful heart, "It has been so long! How can Jehovah allow His people to continue to be oppressed? How long, oh Lord, how long?"

The cry for deliverance that had been repeated by thousands during the long years of waiting sank deep into Benjamin's soul. He, too, waited for the Messiah, but not as those around him. The dreaming nature that thrilled at fiery sunrises and flame-tipped storm clouds set him apart. Abner, Ara, hundreds like them, longed for a king, a ruler who would exalt the seed of David to its rightful place. Benjamin yearned for One to set all people free. The fervor in his soul for those who dwelt in fear and squalor, those forced to bow to Roman rule, rose within him like gorge. Why could not Jews and Romans, Chaldeans and Samaritans and Greeks live together in peace?

Only once had he dared ask Ara that question. His father had proudly drawn himself up. "Jews do not live with Roman dogs. Not until the lion lies down with the lamb shall such a thing be."

"Then I long for that day," Benjamin whispered, eager to remove the hatred from his father's face.

Now he leaned his head back against clasped hands and looked at the lustrous stars. Never had he seen such a display. Something about the night made him feel a day of peace might indeed be possible. His eyes bulged. The stars looked closer moment by moment. "Father, Abner, look." Benjamin leaped up and pointed to a strange, flowing star. "It is growing light."

"It cannot be!" Abner and the others hurried to their feet. "Not at this hour." Yet they spun to look in the direction Benjamin faced. Awe replaced disbelief. Lighter and lighter the night grew. Blue shadows fled from an approaching radiance that bathed the fields in an unearthly glow. The animals showed no fear, even when a figure appeared in the midst of the light, but every shepherd fell to the ground, arms out-stretched. "Mercy. Have mercy upon us!"

Benjamin cowered with the others, hands over his face, yet his fingers could not shut out the light. Never had he been so afraid, not even when a bear or snarling wolf came to the flock and had to be driven away.

A soft voice penetrated his terror. He dared raise his head just enough to see the glowing figure. Was it an angel, such as came and wrestled with Jacob? Nay. Angels did not appear to poor shepherds. Yet what else could it be? He must be dreaming. Benjamin struck his leg hard to prove him-self awake. He saw his father, Abner, and the others, shaking in the light that poured over them.

In a voice beyond description, the angel spoke. "Fear not. I bring you good tidings. Unto you is born this day in the city of David a Savior, which is Christ the Lord. This shall be a sign unto you. You shall find the babe wrapped in swaddling clothes, lying in a manger."

The voice ceased. Before Benjamin could grasp the incredible message or move a muscle, night vanished into brilliance beyond the noonday sun. A great multitude of other heavenly beings joined the angel. "Glory to God in the highest," they sang. "On earth peace, good will to men."

Moments or eternities later, Benjamin could not tell which, the great light slowly began to fade. The heavenly chorus disappeared, its only trace a faint song that dwindled to nothingness. The shepherds looked at one another, curiously, hesitantly. Never in the history of the world had such a thing happened to a band of humble men such as themselves. Had it now, or were they victims of some powerful illusion?

Ara had no doubt. First back on his feet, he bellowed into the night, "Praise the Holy One of Israel, for He has come. Messiah has come!" Great drops rolled down his weather-beaten face. Others took up the cry until the flocks lay massed beneath a gigantic swell of joy.

"We must go find Him," Abner exclaimed, dancing as he had not danced in more years than he could remember. "We must find the babe."

"Yea." Ara's eyes never lost their glow. "We must journey to Bethlehem, the city of David. Angels have proclaimed the Messiah's birth. My soul's prayers have been granted. I shall see the Holy One before I die." Majestic in his finest hour of triumph, Ara more than ever resembled the great beast that had given him his name. "Come, let us not delay."

A quiver of fear brushed Benjamin's mind for the second time that awe-filled night. He impatiently pushed it aside. No time for dreaming, now, with much to be done to secure the sheep.

"The sheep." Benjamin barely spit the words from his dry throat. "Who will care for the sheep?"

Torn from their rejoicing, blank dismay descended like a shroud. No one moved. Happiness receded, leaving visages grim, disappointed. Abner broke the silence. "We could draw lots," he said heavily. His agonized face showed how he dreaded being the one left behind. He threw a few more faggots on the fire. Its quick blaze showed the same expression on each of the faces around Benjamin.

What if Ara, oldest of the shepherds, drew the lot and could not go? Benjamin could not bear the thought. Nor, he discovered the next moment, could he bear to have any of them miss the wondrous happening. He drew a long, quivering breath and shook his mop of curly dark hair. "I will stay. I have waited a lifetime to see the Messiah, but you —" He fixed his gaze on his father. "You have waited two or three of my lifetimes. All of you." He managed to smile even though the sharp sword of disappointment pierced him until he wondered if he could remain brave enough to stay behind. For good measure he added, "When you return from Bethlehem and tell me what you find and where to look, I too will travel to the Christ-child."

The pride that bloomed in Ara's face, the mumbled gratitude from Abner and the others, smothered some of Benjamin's loneliness. What mattered it that time must pass before he reached Bethlehem? Would he not rejoice even more for having waited? Feeling he had chosen the better part, he hastily helped the others herd all the sheep into one giant flock before the men departed. Benjamin waved them out of sight, cheered by Ara's promise, "We shall return soon, son of my right hand. Then you shall surely see the glory of the Lord God Jehovah."

Quiet again descended. Only Benjamin and the large flock inhabited the valley. He slowly walked to the place where the angels had hovered a few hours before, then knelt. For him and his companions, the spot would ever be holy ground. Snatches of the night's happenings returned. Abner, passionately wondering what, if anything, the Messiah had to do with poor shepherds. Ara, face transformed. Himself, offering to remain so his elders might not be denied their greatest dream. Peace blanketed the fields. The flock lay undisturbed. In spite of Benjamin's determination to watch carefully, weariness born of excitement overtook him and he slept.

Hours later, an accusing rosy dawn peered over a low hill. Benjamin sprang from the ground, chagrined. He counted his father's flock, then Abner's and the others'. A prayer of gratitude winged into the morning sky. All there, but what a poor shepherd he was, sleeping while on guard! The great Jehovah who created and loved the animals had protected them.

To his amazement, the day fled before his solitary duties. Many times he found himself turning to question his father before remembering Ara had gone. At sunset he built a small fire and prepared a simple meal: broth, a chunk of meat, bread baked earlier on a flat stone. How different to be alone. Yet how could he feel alone when the memory of the glowing star, the unexplainable light, the angel's message and song danced in the evening dusk and rustled in his mind?

He repeated the message that had eternally burned into his brain, savoring every word until he came to, *You shall find the babe wrapped in swaddling clothes, lying in a manger.*

"A manger?" he cried. "A common feed box for beasts? How can such a thing be? Why is there no place readied for the baby's birth? Even animals seek what shelter they can before birthing their young." Stay. Perhaps no one knew they were coming. Great hordes of persons had swelled the population of the country in the necessity to return to their birth villages to be taxed. Surely the parents wanted a better place for their son than a manger. What a way to welcome the Messiah, who should have been wrapped in royal robes!

Fear smote Benjamin. Jehovah surely would grow angry with the poor welcome and curse those people who had not prepared for the King's coming. The next instant the angel song reassured him. The messengers had been filled with praise and joy. If Jehovah were angry, the angels would not have sung so.

Life among the sheep had given Benjamin much time to ponder and sharpen his perception. Had the angels sung to others? Had they gone from house to house announcing the good news? It hardly seemed possible, yet neither did it seem likely only humble shepherds had been visited and heard the glad song. He remembered how many times Ara had sadly shook his head and said, "Many no longer watch for him. They are downtrodden, discouraged, and have forgotten the promises." Had the angels been unable to find those who still looked for the coming of the Messiah?

If only Ara and his friends would return tonight. Or in the morning. What would they tell of wonders and marvels they might have seen? He would leave as soon as someone came and relieved him. Darkness fell and no one came, but Benjamin did not worry. It might have taken time to find the newborn babe. He rolled himself in a blanket, but this night awakened every few hours to find the sheep peaceful and safe.

For several days he faithfully tended his charges and waited. Then one night when darkness crept near after an incomparable sunset that filled his beauty-loving soul, he heard shouts and ran to meet the men.

Travel-stained, weary, they triumphantly called, "We have seen the Messiah, Benjamin, and life will forever be changed!"

Abner. Jonathan. Simeon. "Where is my father?" Benjamin peered into the shadows, wondering that Ara had not strode forward to greet him.

Abner's heavy hand fell on the boy's shoulder. "He tarried in Bethlehem. He could not bear to leave the place the Promised One was born. You are to leave in the morning and meet him there. He is resting and will come back with you."

On fire with impatience, Benjamin declared, "I will go now."

"Nay." Abner stubbornly shook his head. "Ara says you must not travel at night. We found it difficult to get there. The roads are filled with rough men and night is not safe. Strong as you are, you would be no match for robbers."

Benjamin reluctantly accepted the wisdom of Abner's words. "Tell me, Abner," he pleaded. "Why was the Messiah in a manger?"

The older man hesitated so long, Benjamin ached to prod him the way he sometimes did the donkey Ebenezer who lay sleeping beside the sheep. Abner finally said, "The people of Bethlehem know nothing of what happened here in the fields or in their city. When we asked if anyone had seen angels and heard them sing, they ran from us as if we were mad. We soon learned to hold our tongues."

"We had to find the child." His set jaw showed how none would have returned from a fruitless mission. "We had to be careful when making inquiry, lest we gain the unwelcome attention of Romans by being pointed out as mad. At last we found an innkeeper who appeared strangely upset. Yea, he had turned away many. Yea, his space had been filled with those who carried bags heavy with silver and gold. Yea, he remembered a young man and his wife, weary from the road, the wife heavy with child. But he had no room. He directed them to a clean cave nearby, a warm place with clean straw."

"And a manger," Benjamin put in.

Abner nodded. "At least it got her off the road. The innkeeper said the man seemed grateful and the woman — hardly more than a girl — smiled in a way that made him sorry he had nothing better to offer."

"As he should be," Benjamin growled, and a chorus of assent rose from the other shepherds.

Abner's voice lowered. "We found them. The Messiah had been born, a tiny babe whose little hand we touched when the mother smiled and beckoned us near. I've seen many babies, but not like this one. Joseph and Mary, for those are their names, agreed to allow your father to wrap himself in a blanket and stay in the edge of the cave."

His face fell. "We went through the village and told the people. The few who listened, laughed and threatened to call the guards. The Deliverer lay sleeping in a manger in their town — and they didn't even know it."

"Because He came so simply?"

"It may be so. They weren't expecting Him." He yawned. "Rest, Benjamin. Tomorrow you go to Bethlehem and see for yourself."

Long after the others slept, the youngest shepherd lay huddled in his blanket. The Messiah had come and people didn't recognize Him. What could it mean? How would it end? Exhaustion finally claimed him, but before he fell into slumber, he gazed into the heavens. The stars blurred, forming strange patterns. One was a cross. Too tired to puzzle it out, he slept. In the morning's excitement Benjamin forgot to ask Abner about it.

"Take your faithful donkey Ebenezer," Abner directed. "I will watch your sheep. Ebenezer, 'stone of help' that he is, will carry you to Bethlehem and Ara can ride back, if he chooses." A chill went through Benjamin and changed to foreboding when Abner added, "Hasten. I feel time is important." He raised his hand in blessing, and Benjamin began his journey.

Warm sunlight cheered him. Ebenezer trotted along at a surprisingly good pace, a dumb, gray companion, but one Benjamin loved. It should not take long to reach Bethlehem. A thrill of anticipation went through him. He would find Ara at the cave with the little family. What a reunion with his father that would be, kneeling at the feet of the newborn King! He reached a bend in the road on a hilltop not far from Bethlehem, still dreaming.

"Halt!" The rude order brought him out of his reverie. A band of men rode down an incline toward him. Not Roman soldiers, but dark-faced, raggedy men on half-starved horses as wild-looking as their riders.

Benjamin stopped Ebenezer. His muscles tensed. Sweat trickled beneath his tunic and he desperately looked around for help. The dusty road lay empty except for the flint-eyed men who surrounded him.

two

"Get down, boy." The mean-looking man who evidently led the motley band jerked a dirty thumb toward the ground and glared at Benjamin.

He clutched Ebenezer's mane with stiff fingers. If only help would come!

"Get down, I tell you!" The leader swung a heavy whip to loosen Benjamin's grip. It missed the boy's hands, but hit him full across the temple and knocked him half-senseless to the dusty road.

"You've killed him!" a high-pitched voice screeched. "Ride!"

Through his pain, Benjamin realized the need to lie motionless. A kick from a heavy boot sent him flying to the side of the road, lips clenched to keep back the moan that sprang from his fear-parched throat.

"We'll take the donkey. We need it more than he will." A coarse laugh mingled with

Ebenezer's bray of protest, then thudding hooves. Benjamin slitted his eyes open just enough to see the thieves ride away with poor Ebenezer trotting behind them, held fast by a frayed rope. Why hadn't he played dead, the way he did at home when he didn't want to go? The injured lad struggled to rise, failed, and rolled farther off the road until covering bushes hid his body. His head hit something hard. A fresh burst of pain shot through him, and he knew no more.

"What have we here?" A kindly voice roused Benjamin. He fought through black dizziness and opened his eyes. A man bent above him, hand extended.

"Where am I?" Benjamin gingerly touched his throbbing head.

"A little way from Bethlehem." The man succeeded in getting him to his feet. He led the dazed boy to a rude cart bearing a few wares and motioned him to sit among them. "I am Jonas. My hut is not far."

"Peace be unto you," Benjamin murmured and collapsed under the blanket of darkness that fell over him. When he roused, he wondered at the rough walls around him, the pallet on which he lay. He struggled to sit up, glad his head no longer ached.

"All is well." A gentle hand pressed him back. "My husband found you beside the road, struck down by evil men, no doubt."

"I must go. The child —"

A worry wrinkle crossed the pleasant face. "Jonas found no child."

"The Christ-child, the Messiah. In Bethlehem."

"We will speak of such things when my husband returns." She slipped from his side and returned with a bowl of broth. Spoonful after spoonful slid down his throat, bringing strength to Benjamin's body, reason to his mind.

After Jonas came, he told the good people all that had happened. He watched their eyes open wide in amazement. Would they believe him? By the time he finished his tale, the sun rested on a hill like a golden crown. "I must go. You say it has been many days since you found me." A pang went through him. "Father awaits me in Bethlehem. He will worry."

"You are too weak," Jonas protested. His wizened face brightened. "When you are able, I myself will take you, with great joy."

A few days later they waved farewell to Jonas' wife and started toward Bethlehem with the cart. Once they found the Messiah, Jonas would rush back to tell his wife while Benjamin stayed. At last the belated follower would see the Promised One. Joy beat in his brain, kept time with their slow footsteps. The Messiah. Just ahead. Around the next bend. Over the next hill.

They reached the cave without trouble. Anguish awaited them. It lay empty.

Benjamin longed to drop his head into his hands and weep like a child. How could such a terrible thing happen when he so longed to find the Messiah? Had not the prophet Moses on the plains of Moab stated, "If thou shalt seek the Lord thy God, thou shalt find Him, if thou seek Him with all thy heart and with all thy soul?"

Day after day he and Jonas inquired about those who had dwelt in the cave on the marvelous night. No one knew or cared what had happened to the little family. Neither could he find his father. At last one man scornfully told them, "That crazy shepherd? He went back to his mad friends, or so they say."

"If only I had come sooner," Benjamin wailed.

His disappointment was reflected in Jonas' eyes, but his benefactor quietly reminded him, "You could not help being set upon." He looked toward the west where the sun lingered, as if reluctant to bid the day goodnight. His voice rang like a prophet of old. "One day, my son, you will find Him.

First, go to your father. I am too old to search and I cannot leave the wife of my youth for a long journey. When you find the Messiah, remember an old man who once helped you. Bring me word, if I have not gone on to the land of our fathers."

"I make a vow to do so." Rosy clouds witnessed the clasp of hands before they turned away from Bethlehem, then dusk fell.

The next morning they started back over the dusty road. After Benjamin bade Jonas farewell at the hut, he hurried on as if pursued by a thousand devils. A sense of urgency lent speed to his feet. It increased when he reached the fields and Abner ran to him, dark face set. "Where have you been?" he demanded.

"I was set upon and beaten. Thieves took Ebenezer. Now the manger is empty, the family gone. Where is my father?"

A worry cloud spread over Abner's face. "He is not well. He returned from Bethlehem strangely silent. He wanted to follow the child and His parents but weakness overcame him. He waited and waited for your arrival, so you could go in his place." He motioned to a nearby tent and followed Benjamin inside.

Benjamin found his father reclining on a mat. He could scarcely believe the ravages of nature that had come in such a short time. Only Ara's eyes looked alive. He cried, "My son, you have come." His cracked voice exulted. "I have seen my Lord, Benjamin. I can die with my soul at rest."

"You must not die, my father." Benjamin took the thin hand. "We must follow the Christ-child together."

"We shall follow Him. He is everywhere." A look of mysticism came to the thinned face. "He will be with me when I go, even as He will be here with you. You are young, strong. My son, never stop seeking until you find the Messiah and kneel at His feet, as I have done."

"How can I?" Benjamin bitterly asked, remembering the empty cave. "I am too late. He has gone from Bethlehem."

"I know, but one day you shall find Him."

Benjamin's heart fluttered at the same words Jonas had used, the same assurance. His heart took flight, then missed a beat when his father's eyes closed. How frail and white he looked, but how glorious his face. Ara opened his eyes and gazed through the tent opening. His son had the feeling he saw far beyond the Judaean hills. "Peace to you, Benjamin, son of my right hand. Find and follow Him . . ."

He suddenly sat straight up. His dark eyes

blazed; his face turned radiant. He stretched out both hands. "Yea, I come." For a full minute he sat so, then dropped back. A lamb bleated, stilled. Silence lay heavy in the small tent.

Benjamin could not weep in the presence of such glory. If he reached the age of Methuselah, never would he forget the look on his father's face. Surely he had seen beyond the heavens.

Abner slipped away, leaving father and son. He seized a ram's horn and blew the call to summon the other shepherds. "Ara would not want us to mourn," he told them. "I wish to remain with the boy for a time. I will throw our flocks together."

In the following sad days the crusty shepherd saw to Benjamin. A love much like that he had given his father grew in the grieving lad's heart. For a time after the burial, he simply kept the sheep and ate what Abner set before him. Then one day he told his friend, "I must go."

"Yea." The great-hearted man made no protest. Little of the boy Benjamin remained in the young man who stood before him, tall and determined. "If you are ever in need, come back. Ara's sheep are yours. I will keep an account."

Benjamin shook his curly dark head. "I

have promised my father and Jonas. I shall find the Messiah, even if it takes all the days of my life."

"Peace." Strong hands met in the love shared only by those who have also known sorrow together. Benjamin turned away to hide unmanly tears. He mounted the hill above the only home he had ever known but did not look back. He knew Abner stood where he had left him, solid as a rock in a land grown weary without Ara. Every line of his rigid body shouted his desire to make the quest; regret that his years must keep him tending sheep while his spirit traveled with the lad he loved as a son.

Blinded with emotion, Benjamin set his face toward Bethlehem. He must start with the empty manger. He raised his face to the smiling sky. "I am coming," he called, knowing it would drift back on the early morning breeze to the solitary figure below.

For a single, mad moment he wondered if the old shepherd would spring to leave everything and follow. Benjamin fancied he heard a faint, "Wait for me." He shook his head. Nay. Benjamin set his sandaled feet on the road to find his Lord, leaving Abner with only the sheep and memories of an unforgettable night to heal his aching heart.

Again he longed to look back. He dared

not. The strong cords that bound him to the land where his father lay would tie him with those who must grow old telling tales of the angel song. Always he would wish he had followed. Then, too, there was his promise. Three times he had vowed — to Ara, Jonas, and Abner. He could not embrace the safety of the past. Beckoning roads called, the pull of the unknown. He went down the hill, wishing for his gray friend Ebenezer. "I hope they treat him kindly," he told a passing bird and shifted his awkward bundle of provisions. His feet slowed. No feeling of hurry pervaded him, and he still felt dazed from the past weeks' events.

Eventually, Benjamin rounded the bend in the road that had been his downfall. If he had not been set upon, how different things might have been. The loss of Ebenezer and the lost days in Jonas' hut had proved a stumbling block.

The bushes at the side of the road where he had lain senseless rustled. His heart sank. Surely the great Jehovah would not permit him to be robbed a second time! He refused to look, but kept straight on, head high.

Something poked into his back. He turned. No robber there. Just the grizzled head of a gray donkey who rent the air with glad brays.

"Ebenezer! How can it be?" He hugged his shaggy friend. "Did you play dead after all?" He spied a piece of frayed rope still around the donkey's neck. "Or did you break free?"

Ebenezer brayed again, raucously, joyously, and nudged his master.

"We are going to find the Messiah," Benjamin told him while he transferred his provisions to the donkey's back. Ebenezer cocked one ear. Benjamin had talked to him since they were both small.

"She rode a donkey, just like you," Benjamin went on. "The Christ-child's mother. What need had she of fine horses or camels? Mary probably loved her little donkey." He scratched Ebenezer's head and won a bray of agreement.

Before going into Bethlehem, they stopped to see Jonas. Perhaps he had news. The old man and his wife met them at the door. "So quickly you come! Have you then found the Messiah?" Happiness loomed large on their faces.

"Nay. My father died. I am only starting my journey."

Disappointment shadowed the watching eyes. "It is as I feared. A dream came to me, a city of great beauty. My forefathers awaited me near the gates. I wanted to go inside but said, 'First I must find the Christ-child.'

"A voice spoke, although I saw no one. 'You will find Him, but not where you seek.' I fear the dream warns I am too old and will not see Him in this life."

Sadness gradually faded. "You will find Him. I have learned the family is from Nazareth. They would go there. Then, too, the child must be circumcised on the eighth day, according to the law of Moses. That is past. The mother must pass through the days of purification after the birth of a son. When they are accomplished, the parents must take the baby to Jerusalem and present Him to the Lord. They will offer sacrifices in the temple, a pair of turtle doves or pigeons. You must go to Jerusalem, Benjamin. Surely you will find Him there."

"I will go and when I find Him, I shall return to you. Again I vow." Excitement went through him.

"It will be according to the will of the Lord. If you do not find the little family, those who saw them at the temple will direct you. If it takes longer than we hope, we will wait joyously for you to come to the place we have gone. It makes little difference where we find the Messiah, but that we do. Time is nothing with Jehovah. Only foolish men grow impatient."

Benjamin sang himself hoarse on the journey to Jerusalem. He asked every traveler from the city, "Did you see the baby at the temple?"

Always came a burst of laughter. "I saw many babies at the temple. What name is given to the one you seek?" When Benjamin confessed he did not know, the laughter grew louder. "He seeks a baby whose name is unknown! Can even the gods help him?"

Not the gods, but the true and living God, the inquirer silently replied.

Some eyed him suspiciously. "Why do you seek this child?" They sneered and drew their cloaks around them when he told of the great light and angel message. He learned to keep his own counsel. The great Jehovah must not have told many of His Son's birth. Benjamin continued to question but no longer shared his reason for asking.

One evening when the sun kissed the land farewell, the two weary travelers arrived outside the gates of the city Jerusalem. Never in all of his dreaming had Benjamin known how it would be. The temple, shining and beautiful, turned to molten gold when an errant ray of sunlight outlined it.

He fell to the ground. "Oh, Lord, I praise Thy name." He could say no more. All his life he had heard of the temple but nothing had prepared him. The sun disappeared in a flurry of scarlet banners that reflected on the temple walls and warned the time to seek lodging had come.

Benjamin found rude lodgings nearby. A pittance bought food and shelter for them both. God was good. Never mind the crude abode and coarse fare. Tomorrow he would find the Christ-child. Before the first cock crowed, Benjamin was up and ready to begin searching. He flung his arms around Ebenezer's neck. "You have truly been a stone of help. Rest friend."

After a quick breakfast of bread with small portions of cheese and dates, Benjamin slowly made his way through the throngs at the temple gates. Hawkers sold their wares. Visitors from many lands swarmed. The dream of every Jewish man, woman, and child was to see the temple, the law itself. Robed priests rubbed elbows with fierce desert chiefs. Lofty Romans on horseback towered above the others, spears ready. Where did they all come from, the litters carried by black-skinned men? Sometimes silken curtains shifted to give glimpses of languid occupants. Beggars and blind men. Outcasts at the edge of the city, the dreaded lepers crying, "Unclean!" Men with broken bodies, empty eyes. Women with gaudy clothing that proclaimed their vile profession. Old and young. Rich and poor. And in their midst, a simple shepherd, seeking his Messiah.

He tore his gaze from the sights and began to search, feeling he would know the one he sought. The Lord God of Israel would see to it. Again he faced stony stares, suspicion, hatred. The day lengthened and died. He grew desperate and finally sought comfort from Ebenezer when he could not sleep. "There are so many people. Have they not yet come? I have little money. If I sleep with you, my friend, we can stay longer. There is no shame. The Messiah was born in a stable, was He not?"

The next morning his host scowled with suspicion, but seeing his guest's open expression and learning how little means he had, he agreed. "No charge for sleeping in the stable. You will pay only for what you and your donkey eat."

"Peace be upon your house." The surprise in the man's face prompted Benjamin to tell his story. The rough man offered help.

"There is a certain Simeon, a devout man. I have heard it said the Holy Ghost came upon him and revealed he would not taste death before seeing the Messiah. I will take you to him this day."

Never had hours limped by as on that day.

When evening fell, the big man took Benjamin to Simeon and respectfully waited outside in the darkness. The searcher tapped, fingers trembling. Something in Simeon's candle-lit face caused Benjamin to say, "I seek the Christ-child."

"Why?"

Benjamin told the story, seeing understanding in the aged eyes and the sympathy that replaced it. "They were here. All my life I waited, wondering when Messiah would come. After being told it would come to pass and I would behold Him, I waited again. One day the Spirit led me to the temple. A pure, beautiful woman and a strong man had brought their little son to fulfill the law. I took him, not knowing it was — He." Tears fell like rain.

"His name is Jesus. I blessed Him and cried out, 'Lord, now let Thy servant depart in peace . . . mine eyes have seen Thy salvation . . . prepared before the face of all people, a light to lighten the Gentiles, and the glory of Thy people Israel.'"

Benjamin saw in his face a glory like unto that of the heavenly messengers sent to the fields. Ecstasy crowded his throat. How similar were Simeon and Ara — once they had seen the Messiah, life itself paled by comparison.

Simeon spoke of how he warned the mother a sword would pierce her soul. Benjamin burst out, "The cross. I lay looking into the heavens. Suddenly the stars appeared to take the form of a cross."

"I am old and tired. I know of no cross. Go to the temple, my son. Speak with Anna the prophetess. She serves night and day with fasting and prayers. She also saw the child." He raised his arms in a blessing of peace.

Benjamin stumbled out and poured his story into his waiting host's ears on their way back through narrow, sleeping streets. He lay awake until morning, then hurried to find Anna. She proved to be the oldest person he had ever seen, with seamed cheeks and wrinkled forehead. Yet the sunken eyes gleamed with living fire when she said, "Yea, I saw the Messiah and gave thanks unto the Lord. I spake of Him to all them who looked for redemption in Jerusalem." She blessed him, even as Simeon had done.

He dared not ask how long it would be before he found the Messiah but leaped with joy when his host said he had learned the family meant to return to Nazareth, where the father Joseph worked as a carpenter. "If you find Him, will you send word?"

"I shall." Another vow. Hills to climb.

Unfriendly Samaritans, whose land he must cross. How long would it be before he could keep those vows? Benjamin reached the hillside above Jerusalem, stopped Ebenezer, and gazed down. Ominous clouds had risen over Jerusalem. The blackest rested over the temple, as if a great shadow threatened the heart of the Jewish nation. Wind rose, screaming with a hundred voices. Was it a warning? Sometimes the heavens foretold coming events. Bethlehem lay much closer than Nazareth. Perhaps they should go there first.

Ebenezer took a few steps away from the storm. Benjamin shrugged, secretly relieved. Heart far lighter than the lowering sky, he followed the plodding donkey down the dusty road that led to Nazareth.

three

Old Miriam sat weaving in her humble abode, heart bitter as the meaning of her name. How lovely her granddaughter would look robed in the lovely fabric beneath her gnarled fingers. The fingers stilled. A grimace that served as a smile touched the crone-like face. Instead of gracing slim, yet softly rounded Michal, the shimmering folds must drape a fat cow who waddled when she walked the proper distance behind her arrogant husband!

Miriam sighed. If only she could scrape together a dowry. She shook her covered head. How could she, when they barely subsisted on the meager earnings she and Michal brought in with their handiwork? Not that she would have it otherwise. She loved the girl above everything else on earth.

Now she snorted in disgust, making the shuttle fly. "Not one man in this miserable village of Nazareth is worthy of Michal," she declared. She thought of the years she had cared for Michal, whose father died before seeing the child he longed for and whose mother, Miriam's only daughter, died soon after the birth, leaving Miriam alone to protect the beloved child. Unbreakable bonds bound Michal and her grandmother. They had been happy in spite of having little — until now.

Helplessness swept over Miriam, fear of the future. She dropped her hands from the loom and clasped them in prayer. "God of Abraham, Isaac, and Jacob, must the loveliest girl in Nazareth be given to a toadlike Darius?" she cried. "Is it not better for Michal to remain unwed than to become one with the wealthy merchant who covets her? I am old. Soon I go to my reward, whatever it may be. If she is left alone, will not the beauty Thou hast given her become a curse, luring men who care nothing for her purity? How can I sleep in peace without knowing Michal has a strong man to protect her? Hear Thy servant, oh Lord, and grant a blessing, not for my sake, but for hers."

A laughing voice outside the open door broke into her plea. Miriam hastily wiped her eyes on the sleeve of her rough garment so in contrast with the fine fabric she wove. Michal must not find her weeping. She took up the shuttle and bent her head to hide traces of her tempest.

The girl who burst into the room had little thought for sadness, much for the joy that comes from youth, a strong body, and mind, and devotion to the Creator. The old woman's heartbeat quickened. She forgot the danger that came with shining dark brown hair under a simple veil, glowing brown eyes, and skin that never coarsened. Sixteen winters and summers had passed since Miriam delivered the perfect girl child and announced, "She shall be called Michal. It means 'who is like the Lord?' I shall guard her with my life, if need be." The innocence in the laughing face sent a thrill of pride through Miriam and a silent prayer winged its way upward.

"I bring good news." Michal's laughter rang like the temple bells Miriam had heard when she visited Jerusalem long ago. She held out a shapely, well-cared-for hand. "See? Darius, miser that he is, paid more than we expected." She dropped a small amount of coins in Miriam's hand, then placed her hands on her hips, arms akimbo. Mischief lurked in the depths of her clear eyes. "I told him Miriam the weaver is the best in Nazareth and unless he wishes to be accused of usury, he must give us a fair price."

"You dared?" Miriam inwardly rejoiced yet refrained from outwardly approving. The extra coins would buy a small luxury or two they usually could not afford. Yet if Michal had looked as beautiful defying Darius as she did now, woe unto them! What man could gaze on such a one and not desire her?

"Yea. It is time the villagers stopped abasing themselves before him." She swept low in obeisance and mimicked those who fawned on anyone with wealth. "So be it, worthy Darius. Thou art wise and good, far wiser than your humble servants deserve. Have mercy on us, oh mighty one." In her normal voice she added contemptuously, "One would think him second in command to the great Jehovah. Not I." Her naturally red lips twisted in scorn. "He thinks because he has riches people will forget he came of miserable parents who deserted him when he was still a boy. If a passing caravan had not taken pity on him, Darius would have died. How did he reward them? If village tales are to be believed, he stole all he could easily carry and fled. Darius is not his real name, you know. He took it because it

46

means wealth in Greek and that is all he cares about."

"Have you never longed for riches, my child?" Miriam held her breath.

Michal rid herself of the veil and vigorously shook her head. "Has not the great God given us all we need? Food, shelter, and each other. All is ours." A mist shone in her eyes and her face glowed. "Has He not also promised to send a deliverer when the time is right? Why should we care for anything else?"

"Not even a strong, young man for you?"

A lovely pink stained the smooth face. "Why, Grandmother! Never have you spoken of such a thing." A little smile trembled on her lips, showing her not as indifferent to the idea as she might be.

"Some of your friends are already betrothed, some married." Miriam anxiously watched the girl. "Is not Mary soon to wed Joseph, the carpenter?"

Happiness over extracting a more just payment from Darius fled, leaving Michal's cheeks pale. She sank to a stool near the loom and shook her head. "I know not."

"I thought the arrangements had been made." Miriam watched Michal in surprise. What could bring such a strange look to her beloved child's face?

"There are strange stories in the village." Each word came out as if wrenched free from a wondering heart. "People are whispering that — that Mary is not a good girl."

"Gossip is seldom to be believed," Miriam reminded. "I know of no maidens more modest than Mary and you. What can the tale-bearers say about such a one? Why, I have known her parents all the days of my life, Mary as well. Surely this is unkind and idle gossip." When Michal didn't answer, her grandmother said sharply, "What else do they say?"

Red flags waved in Michal's face. "That . . . that she is with child." She leaped to her feet. "It cannot be. She is good! I know. Yet it is said Joseph himself is mindful to put her away privily. He is a just man and not willing to make her a public example." Tears glittered. One rolled. Then another.

"Have you spoken with Mary?" Miriam clenched her hands.

"How can I, about such a thing?" Michal dashed away tears. "It would seem I question her virtue. Oh, Grandmother, how can people be so cruel?" She collapsed back on the stool. "I know in my heart Mary is pure, yet when I said so at the well, many of the women raised their eyebrows and smiled unpleasantly. What can I do?" She buried her face in her hands.

"Remain loyal to your friend." Miriam rested her workworn hand on the young girl's bent head and stroked the tangled curls. Yet her heart lay inside her heavy as a stone. The ways of the Evil One were many. Had he tempted Mary? How could it be, if Joseph knew nothing about it? The thought gave her comfort. "Michal, who is doing the most whispering?"

"Naomi and Abigail," came the muffled reply.

"I am not surprised. Both coveted Joseph the carpenter, if my memory serves me well. They were enraged when he chose Mary. I myself heard their mothers state Joseph should have chosen someone nearer his own age — meaning one of their daughters."

Michal raised a radiant face. "Then it is all the work of jealous women?"

"I know not. I do know Mary cannot be what they say. Michal, I do not believe in listening to tales, but I want you to know the truth. Listen to all you hear, but do not speak in anger. Bring the news to me. We will decide what we can do to best help Mary, poor child. It is a terrible thing to be the object of a village's scorn."

"The charges are false," Michal whispered. She laid a hand over her tunic that rose and fell with the quick beat of her heart. "Then why do I grieve? Is my faith in Mary so weak I cannot trust her fully?"

Miriam prayed for guidance. She must say just the right thing. "One day you shall surely know the truth and when you do, all doubt will flee."

"I pray the day will come soon." The words were so low Miriam had to strain to hear them. The next moment Michal took a long breath and said, "I will prepare our evening meal, Grandmother." She spread a small cloth on a table nearby, cut bread and cheese, and poured each a half cup of precious goat's milk. After a simple blessing, they ate. Neither referred again to Mary.

In the next weeks and months tiny whispers changed to a mighty roar. The news about Mary and Joseph swept into every narrow street, every hovel and shop in Nazareth. Some said an angel with a flaming sword appeared to Joseph in a dream and told him Mary was pure and he need not fear to take her. Others said there was no flaming sword at all. Strange stories about the child everyone knew she now carried ran rampant. Michal and Miriam trembled and at last the old woman bade her granddaughter to go to Mary.

"Everyone knows she is with child," she reasoned. "It is better for you to assure her you know she is pure and openly ask for the truth than to refrain from discussing this thing, although it is not our custom to speak of such matters."

At first Michal demurred, but she had postponed a visit far too long. Mary had been home some time after a three-month visit in the hill country city of Juda with her cousin Elisabeth, wife of Zacharias. Surely she must wonder why Michal had not come.

One sunny afternoon Michal put on her nicest clothing, covered her hair modestly with a veil, and went to her friend. She clenched her fingers and tried to will her fearful heart to be still. How could she refer to what lay uppermost in her mind without causing Mary further pain?

She had no need to fear. Once seated, Mary looked deep into Michal's eyes and the visitor had her answer. No one on earth who broke the commandments of the living God could wear such an exalted expression. Mary resembled Michal's idea of what angels must look like, with things of the spirit far outweighing the physical body.

"I have a story to tell you, Michal. Never in the world has such a thing come to pass.

The prophets foretold it, yet had it not happened to me I would find it hard to believe." Her face glowed with an unearthly light. "My sister, I bear witness to you. Every word I tell you is true."

Relief filled Michal and she impulsively clasped both Mary's hands in hers. "I am so glad! I knew you weren't — you couldn't — but how . . . ?" She broke down.

Mary smiled. "In the sixth month while I was espoused to Joseph, but before we came together as man and wife, an angel of God came to me." At Michal's start of surprise, her grip tightened. "Nay, I had never seen an angel, yet I could not but know he was one. I cannot say how. He said to me, 'Hail, thou that art highly favored, the Lord is with thee: blessed art thou among women.'

"I could not understand why he should greet me so, a humble virgin of Nazareth. It troubled me, but the angel said, 'Fear not, Mary: for thou hast found favor with God. And, behold, thou shalt conceive in thy womb, and bring forth a son, and shalt call His name Jesus.'"

Michal gasped. Her heart thumped. Her eyes burned and something within her stirred, not belief, but the desire to believe.

Mary's eyes held compassion. "I know you find it difficult to understand. So did I.

The angel said the child would be great and called the Son of the Highest, that the Lord God would give unto Him the throne of His father David. He said the child should reign over the house of Jacob forever and of His kingdom there would be no end. Like you, I knew such a thing could not happen. I said to the angel, 'How shall this be, seeing I know not a man?'" Her fingers loosened and fell back to rest on her swollen belly. Awe crept into her eyes, as if even yet she could not comprehend the magnitude of what had happened all those weeks before.

"What did he say?" Michal felt the whole world waited for the answer.

" 'The Holy Ghost shall come upon thee, and the power of the Highest shall over- shadow thee: therefore also that holy thing which shall be born of thee shall be called the Son of God,'" she quoted.

Michal's mind whirled, torn between rea- son and the truth in Mary's voice. She could not speak.

"The angel, who was Gabriel, must have sensed how I struggled. He told me my cousin Elisabeth, long past the age for child- bearing, had conceived a son in her old age; that she who had been called barren was in her sixth month. He said that with God, nothing is impossible. I do not know what caused me to cry out, but I said, 'Behold the handmaid of the Lord: be it unto me according to thy word.' The angel departed and I was alone with the greatest joy a woman can know, nay, joy beyond that. Who was I to be the mother of God's own Son?"

"I know of no one more fitting." Michal's heart felt full to the bursting point. She knelt before her friend and blindly groped for her hand.

"Do not bow to me, my sister, only to the Lord God on high." Mary gently drew her up. "I am merely a vessel to carry the Chosen One."

"The Messiah?" Michal breathed, heart aflame.

"Not everything has been given to me to know." Mary's face settled into sadness. "Michal, there is more. Joseph did not understand. What man could?"

"They said in the village he had a dream." Michal wished she could take back the words. Mary must be all too aware of Nazareth gossip.

Her friend smiled again, a golden look Michal had seen before in the faces of those who first held their newborn babies. "It is true. God knew of Joseph's ponderings and sent an angel as a witness of the truth, that this is of God. He told Joseph, 'She shall bring forth a son, and thou shalt call His name Jesus: for He shall save His people from their sins.'"

"Jehovah must love Joseph and trust him very much to choose Him to be the child's earthly father," Michal whispered.

A great light came to Mary's eyes, but she only nodded before continuing the most amazing, wonderful story Michal had ever heard. "After the angel left it seemed like a dream. Time passed. I decided to rise and go to Elisabeth, for the angel had said she was in her sixth month. She met me at the door. I learned the babe leaped in her womb when I came. She greeted me and in a loud voice asked how it was the mother of her Lord should come to her. Then the babe in my own womb leaped for joy and I said, 'My soul doth magnify the Lord, and my spirit hath rejoiced in God my Saviour . . .'"

Mary's voice went on in a song of praise. It fell on deaf ears. Michal had heard so much that could not be explained, she could not in take any more. Mary finished, "I came home after three months. Now I must wait." A gentle smile and a loving pat on Michal's hand followed, along with a final remark. "There are those who say I made up the story. Some would take and stone me if it were not for Joseph. Dear friend who has been as a sister to me, ponder these things in your heart as I have done. You cannot help but know they are true. Peace and grace be unto you."

Still dazed, Michal left Mary's home. She walked right past Naomi and Abigail, gossiping at the village well. She didn't see Darius, who lounged in the entrance to his shop and devoured her with his greedy gaze. Even the small, ragged children who clamored for stories and usually got them danced around her in vain. She must get to Miriam and proclaim the good news. The angel had said Jesus would save His people from their sins. He must be the Messiah.

Miriam breathlessly drank in every word, faithfully repeated by the girl who felt they had been etched into her brain forever. After her initial protest, "A child, born of a virgin?" she made no further interruption. When Michal ran out of breath at the end of the story, silence hung between them. At last the old woman looked deep into the brown eyes so like her own had once been, filled with dreams and the ability to accept the miraculous. Oh, to regain her lost youth, the unswerving loyalty to another in trouble, even to the point of rejecting reason.

"Do you believe Mary's story?" she asked.

"I do. It is against all creation but I feel it

in my soul. Grandmother, think what it means. The prophet Isaiah said a virgin would conceive and bear a son. She would call His name Immanuel. Mary's boy child must truly be the Promised One."

"God with us," Miriam translated. She hesitated. "There are those who will say Mary claims to be the one in the prophecy to escape shame."

"They are wrong!" All doubt fled. With knowledge came freedom. "Even in telling the story to you I have learned it is true. I must rush back and tell Mary."

"Dusk is near. Can you not wait until the morn?"

"Nay." Michal knelt beside Miriam. A rush of sympathy came to her expressive face. "How hard it must be for Mary, treasuring all these things in her heart yet being despised by the very ones whose lives can never be the same once her Son is born!" A consciousness of the pain that comes with womanhood twisted her face, compassion and understanding far beyond her years. "Grandmother, think what it would be like — if it were me." Her lips trembled.

"Go, child, and take with you the peace of Miriam," the weaver choked out. "This day has greatness come to Nazareth, lowly and mean as it is. We know not why God's Son will be born to one of our own, but tell Mary she is blessed."

Again Michal flew down the street, not heeding those she met.

Naomi and Abigail spied her from a doorway where they lingered in the hope a young man might pass before darkness drove them to their homes. "Haughty piece." Naomi sniffed.

"I don't see why," Abigail sneered. She flounced her elaborate silk stole. It did little to hide a body made shapeless by lack of work and many sweetmeats. "That old crone she lives with can give her no dowry. Miriam will do well to arrange a marriage with Darius, who pants after Michal. He's positively disgusting and older than Methuselah." She shuddered delicately. "I would open my veins before becoming his wife."

"I, too. Praise be that our parents will find suitable husbands for us," Naomi rejoiced, not adding both had already passed the young age most desirable to prospective bridegrooms. "Here she comes. Now we will have some fun." Naomi stepped directly into Michal's path and said in a honeyed voice, "I see you have been visiting Mary. Tell us, Michal, is she well?"

The girl's spite could not dispel the radiance that clung to Michal like a butterfly clings to the cocoon it discards just before flight. "Mary has never been better. What a wonderful day this is for Nazareth." She stepped around Naomi and went on, leaving the two tormentors gaping and wondering if she had gone mad.

four

Every long, weary mile from Jerusalem to Nazareth, Benjamin thought how difficult the miles must have been for Joseph, knowing his young wife's time of delivery drew near. How much more so for the little mother, great with child. Had they stopped to rest under the spreading arms of the tree where Benjamin chewed dates and Ebenezer dozed, one drooping ear showing how tired he had grown? Or quaffed their thirst from goatskin water bags and longed for villages with wells of fresh, clean water?

"Their dream called them on," Benjamin whispered to Ebenezer. "As it does me. Ah, my friend, you have no dream of the Messiah. Little donkeys simply go where their masters lead." He laughed. "You know of the Messiah, though. Have I not poured out the story into your drooping ears many times on this endless journey?"

Ebenezer pushed closer against his owner, nudged him with his grizzled head, and brayed. He scrambled to his feet at Benjamin's command, refreshed by the midday halt, and the two companions trudged on. In spite of the young man's concern, they had encountered no trouble. Each morning he asked the great God to protect them. Every evening he rejoiced and thanked Him for His care.

Even endless journeys eventually come to a close. Travel-stained and exhausted, the searchers rode into the tiny village of Nazareth in Galilee, a byword in the land. It was said only the offscouring of the earth existed there. Roman soldiers and leaders who displeased the emperor were ordered to Nazareth, a fate filled with ignominy and considered just short of execution.

Benjamin's first joy of discovery had tempered to determination. Where should he start looking for the Messiah? Surely everyone here knew Mary and Joseph. "I will go from hut to hut, shop to shop if I must," he told Ebenezer. Sharp memories of the hostile, suspicious stares received when questioning others in the past checked his eagerness. Caution would be the better way.

Directly ahead stood the village well, central meeting place. Two youngish women, both richly dressed, stood beside it, although flickering shadows warned night drew nigh. One loomed tall and thin, the other short and round as Ebenezer before they started their journey. The pair did not resemble the women who plied their trade on the streets of Jerusalem, yet why were they at the well so late? Perhaps things were different in Nazareth.

Benjamin strode toward them, longing to pour out a hundred questions. Custom checked his tongue. Any conversation beyond a simple greeting might bring down the wrath of their fathers. He smiled, aware of his disheveled condition. "Peace."

"Peace unto you," they chorused. He heard their muffled laughter and felt color rise to his cheeks. Drawing a bucket of water, again and again he dipped his hands into it, cupped them full, and let Ebenezer drink. He drew another bucket of water and drank deeply before splashing water over his hot face. Last of all, he ran wet fingers through his curly black hair, aware of the close scrutiny of the two young women.

"Have you come far?" the taller one inquired.

"From Jerusalem." Glad she had initiated conversation, he added, "I come seeking the Messiah."

"Messiah! In Nazareth?" The second lingerer made a rude sound. "Have you not heard the saying, Can anything good come out of Nazareth?'" She laughed, a jeering sound echoed by her companion. Her blackcurrant eyes looked small in her doughy face. "The day a Messiah comes to Nazareth is the day the Jewish nation eats swine in its unwashed hands!"

Benjamin drew himself to full height and looked straight into the woman's face. He saw reluctant admiration creep into her eyes and wondered. Living among the sheep had not prepared him to deal with women, especially ones like these. Yet the respect he had been given as Ara's son had armed him well. "Know you not that Mary and Joseph from this village traveled to Bethlehem, where they had a child?" He bit his tongue to hold back a torrent of words. Already the expressions on the watching faces had changed.

Never had he seen such a vindictive look as the one the taller woman wore. "Who does not know Joseph the carpenter? As for Mary . . ." She spat out a word that made Benjamin flinch. "She has brought shame to the entire village. Mary! Pretending to be so pure, while all the time she —"

"You are wrong, Naomi." A soft but firm voice from behind Benjamin cut into the diatribe. "Why do you and Abigail hate her so?"

He whirled and looked straight into the loveliest face he had ever beheld. Great dark eyes, large in the pure oval face, gazed from beneath a veil over dark brown hair that rippled like a brook. She appeared much younger than the other two and worlds above them, although garbed in a coarse, woven robe made even rougher by comparison with the silken garments of those she admonished. She carried a heavy bucket on one arm.

"How dare you speak to me like that, Michal? Why does the granddaughter of the weaver crone Miriam, who everyone knows has lived too many days, challenge me?" Naomi drew her rustling skirts closer to her abnormally tall body.

"You would uphold Mary," Abigail sneered. Ugly dull red suffused her skin in great blotches. "May Jehovah forgive you." Her eyes slitted in a cunning look. "Perhaps you should not be blamed," she added sweetly. "Anyone who believes a virgin can conceive and still be spotless as Mary claims is madder than she."

"She would have been stoned if Joseph had accused her instead of pitying her and taking her as his wife in spite of her sin,"

Naomi put in. The corners of her mouth tipped down. "She bewitched him. Imagine him thinking the God of Abraham would send an angel to a humble carpenter. And in Nazareth!" Bitter laughter rent the still and cooling air.

Benjamin's heart leaped with joy. He spoke for the first time. "No more so than angels coming to shepherds in a field."

Naomi clutched Abigail's arm. Fear shone in her eyes. "He is mad, too. Come. We must flee before the demons enter us, as well." They gathered their long skirts and awkwardly ran down the street, leaving Benjamin and the girl called Michal alone except for faithful Ebenezer. He saw the struggle in her face born of modesty, custom, and the desire to ask what he meant.

"I am Benjamin Bar-Ara of Judaea. I seek the Messiah."

Radiance swept into her face. She started to speak, but was interrupted by a querulous cry from an open doorway a little way down the street. "Michal, bring the water." An old woman stepped outside and started toward them. "Who is that with you? You have been taught better than to gossip at the well at eventide, especially with a stranger." Disapproval oozed with every word.

"It is all right, Grandmother. He is Jewish,

like us, and from Judaea." Michal hastily dropped her bucket into the well. He sprang to raise it, filled and dripping. Over her protests, he carried it the short distance to where the old woman still stood, suspiciously peering. Ebenezer ambled along behind.

"Peace be unto you," he greeted. "I come seeking the Christ-child, born in Bethlehem to Mary and to Joseph, the carpenter from Nazareth."

A great change went over Miriam's face. A clawlike hand clutched Benjamin's wrist. "Enter our humble abode, Benjamin Bar-Ara. I would speak with you. Forgive my lack of welcome. I thought you one of the village louts who follow and torment Michal. How good to meet one of our own kind! We, too, came from Judaea, long ago. So long I can remember little except the glory of the temple in the rising sun."

"As I saw it when I left Jerusalem." Benjamin's fine dark brows knitted into a straight line. "Good mother, I also saw dark clouds hanging over the city. Allow me to care for my friend Ebenezer and find lodging. I shall return and tell you what I have learned."

"Pah, you will find no decent lodging here," she sputtered. "We cannot offer you shelter, but there is a shed nearby, empty since Darius the merchant claimed old Matthias' only cow."

"I thank you," he gratefully told her. "I have a flock of sheep near Bethlehem, kept by an old friend, but I carry little substance for fear of thieves."

A short while later, bathed in water carried from the well and wearing a fresh tunic, Benjamin sat with Miriam and Michal. He began his story with the night the angels sang, heart thrilling as it had been. No skepticism showed in either of the attentive faces. Gladness transformed them. He told how he had missed seeing the Christ-child when circumstance forced him to become a belated follower. He relived his meetings with Simeon and Anna.

At this point, Miriam clasped her hands in praise. "I, too, have lived to see glory," she said through her tears. "Benjamin Bar-Ara, the great God has brought you to us this day."

He looked closely at her, not fully understanding, but continued his story. "Those women at the well. What they said about Mary . . ." He floundered.

"It is false," Michal fiercely told him. "The child she bore is a miracle, sent by Jehovah to save us."

"Then He is the Deliverer." Benjamin wanted to shout, to start posthaste back over the long miles. So many awaited the news: Jonas, Abner, the kind host in Jerusalem. And yet — "Are they here?"

"Oh, no." Michal's eyes rounded. "No one in Nazareth has seen them since they rode away to Bethlehem to be taxed, according to the law of Caesar Augustus. They are continually in our prayers and we long for their return. Surely when they come Naomi, Abigail, nay all of Nazareth must recognize the gossip concerning Mary is cruel and untrue."

"Where can they be?" Benjamin cried. "I must kneel at the Messiah's feet and worship Him, as my father Ara, Abner, and the other shepherds did the night of His birth."

"We know not." Miriam's face furrowed into deep valleys. "If He truly is the Promised One as we believe, there will be those who hate and fear Him. His life may be in danger. 'Tis well, I think, for us not to speak of it too loudly. What will you do now, my son? One day Mary, Joseph, and the child surely will come back to Nazareth. Why not remain here for a time? You can find work. I have heard it said that since Joseph left there is need for carpenters. Can you do such work?"

"I can try. I am strong and willing to learn."

He repeated the words the next day to a bent old man drowning in unfinished orders from impatient customers. Soon he could handle wood and tools well, and he enjoyed what he did.

Benjamin would rather have gone into the fields to tend sheep, but feared the family might come and go again while he was out in the fields. He must not miss the Messiah again. At times he wondered, *Should I have gone back to Bethlehem instead of coming here?* He voiced his feelings to old Miriam.

"My son, perhaps you came here for a different reason." The weaver smiled and glanced through the open door at Michal, hastening home from an errand. "I see tenderness in your eyes when you watch her. And in hers, for you. Never has it been there for another man. Benjamin Bar-Ara, it is well you came. I remember a handsome stranger who came to my village long years ago and our happiness together."

Benjamin didn't reply, yet the moment became a turning point. He examined his heart and found it filled with Michal. Her pure face danced between him and his work.

He noticed how her gaze brightened and warm color flushed her cheeks when he came. He heard her singing as she went about the hundred tasks necessary to survive and longed to cast his lot with her and Miriam.

At this point in his thinking, Benjamin always faltered. What right had he to take a wife, when he had vowed to find the Messiah? Reason argued, *it may be years.* Soon Miriam will be gone. Who will protect this child of God from such as Darius, whose face fills with lust when she passes by? From the depths of his soul Benjamin cried, "Oh, Lord, what would You have me do?"

Peaceful weeks later, he stood at the well at sunset, drawing water for Michal. Laughter issued from the shops and dwelling places close by. When they turned toward the hut and Miriam, who awaited them, sadness crept into Benjamin's heart. "Michal," he said abruptly. "I must go away."

She halted and stood immovable as Mount Sinai on which Jehovah had given Moses the law that would last forever. A tiny pulse beat in her white temple, the only sign of agitation save for a flash of fear in her clear, brown eyes.

"I have learned to care for you in these

months since I came to Nazareth." His dark eyes pleaded for understanding, and he touched the sleeve of her garment. "There is another I love even more and I have promised —"

She stepped back and he felt a wall rise between them, higher than those that guarded Jerusalem. "Why did you not tell me?"

"I did, Michal." He stared at her. "The very first night I came. Do you not remember how I vowed to find the Messiah and serve Him all the days of my life?" He could not believe she had forgotten. He saw color rush into her face, the glitter of tears. Understanding came. He took her hand, heedless of possible watching eyes. "Forgive me, beloved. I am as thickheaded as Ebenezer. Do you think I belong to another woman? Nay! My vow is to my God. Even if the days of my life go far past three score and ten, I shall never love anyone on earth as I do you." His voice rang in the quiet street.

Her hand trembled in his. Benjamin bent near to catch her low words. "Think you I would ever stand in the way of your keeping your promise to your God? Oh, Benjamin, how little you know me!"

His jaw set in a stubborn line, although he longed to embrace her. "It would not be fair.

Suppose we became as one and I learned where I could find the Messiah? What then? Already I have missed Him not one, but two times. Yet how could I leave you?"

The anguish in his voice reflected in Michal's eyes. "Benjamin Bar-Ara, what matters it how long you took? One day you would return and find me waiting. Or, if Miriam has gone before us, I would follow you in your quest."

"Nay, you shall walk beside me, not follow," he quickly assured. The simplicity of her answer blotted out his doubts. "May I speak with Miriam?" He laughed. "Leave the future in the hands of Jehovah. Is it not enough that we are pledged, standing by the well in the middle of Nazareth?"

"With Naomi and Abigail observing us," she murmured and demurely freed her hand, then stepped a few paces away from him.

"And Darius." Benjamin scowled at the frowning merchant who boldly returned his stare from his position in front of his shop, arms crossed and wearing a haughty expression.

Great was the rejoicing in the little hut that night. The affection in Miriam's voice when she welcomed Benjamin as a son made him ashamed of how he had once thought her bitter. "It is well," she told the young couple, a worn hand on each of their heads in blessing. "The Lord God of Israel has dealt kindly with me. I will make haste with preparations for the marriage." She laughed, the first time Benjamin had heard her do so, and her sunken eyes twinkled. "Because we are poor, little will be expected of us."

Not long after, Benjamin and Michal became husband and wife in a simple, but moving ceremony. No further word of Mary, Joseph, or the child born in Bethlehem came to their ears. Benjamin worked early and late in the carpenter shop and one day moved his little family to a larger cottage furnished with hand-hewn pieces and love.

A year passed. Michal at last understood the radiance in Mary's face so long ago. Her hand rested on a carefully created cradle, soon to hold the child she carried beneath her heart. Had any woman ever been more blessed than she? Benjamin's love and protection surrounded her like a warm shawl and her feelings for him continued to deepen with each passing day.

Later, Michal wondered if their joy affronted Fate. That very night, Benjamin cried out in his sleep. "Nay. You must not!" He sat bolt upright, sweat pouring from his contorted face.

"Benjamin, what is it?" Michal roused him to awareness.

He shook his tousled, curly head. "I know not, but I am filled with alarm. Something is happening in Jerusalem. I must rise and go. I fear what I may find! The same cloud I saw when I left hangs over the city, yet the blackest part hovers above Bethlehem." He left the bed and lighted a small lamp.

Michal was stricken, but she refused to show it. Benjamin could never journey to Bethlehem and be back by the time of her delivery. Yet she would not, could not hold him. Dreams often presaged coming events. "Go quickly, beloved."

He paused in the act of lacing his sandals, the present replacing the future he dreaded. "How can I go — now?"

"You must. The same Jehovah who guides your footsteps will care for me. Miriam has brought many children into the world. When my days are accomplished, she will bring ours." Michal smiled, knowing she must be strong. "See, it is nearly daylight. Pack Ebenezer, grown fat and lazy in the little pasture behind our home. He has had a long rest, with only trips to the well for water or bearing the burdens of your trade for short distances. The village children who sometimes sit on his back pet and love him. Now he must carry you swiftly."

Ebenezer promptly responded to the packs by lying down and trying his old play dead trick. It worked no better with Benjamin than it ever had. "Come, old friend, we must go to Bethlehem," his master said. One ear drooped, but Ebenezer brayed and raised it when Michal threw her arms around his grizzled neck and something wet and salty fell on his nose.

"Take good care of him, little friend," she whispered. Taking a deep breath she raised her head. "Peace be with you, my husband."

"Peace be upon you, my wife." The look in his face more than rewarded her for holding back the words stored behind her teeth, the plea that he stay with her in her time of need. Until he rode out of sight, she remained where she stood, arm upraised. The next instant she turned to Miriam.

"Grandmother, you must help me. The child will be born soon."

"Michal! I will rouse an urchin and send him after Benjamin."

"Nay. He must go. Michal grimaced in pain and crossed her hands over her swollen belly. "The Lord God will preserve us, even though the babe comes before its time." She staggered inside and to bed.

Miriam heated pots of water, praying

audibly. She thanked God for keeping Benjamin safe and that a new life would soon enter the world. Michal took comfort from the words until a red haze of pain overcame her and she sank into a dark pit from which there seemed no escape.

The travail ended. Miriam brought forth a tiny infant with powerful lungs. "Jehovah be praised! He is small but strong." She finished her work, wrapped Michal's firstborn, and laid him in her arms. "See? He is beautiful."

"He is very red." Michal lay exhausted from her labor.

"That will pass. What is he to be called?" Miriam stroked the fuzz of dark hair on the perfectly formed head, a promise of black curls to come.

Michal gazed at the child at her breast. A swell of love for the helpless scrap of humanity made her feel more complete than ever before in her life. "He is Ara, the lion," she slowly said. "One day he will become strong, like his grandfather and father before him." She fell asleep, with Miriam's thanks unto the Lord for entrusting Ara to their keeping ringing in her ears.

five

Never had Benjamin urged Ebenezer forward at such a rapid pace as on the journey back to Bethlehem. Worn and anxious, they paused at the home of the Jerusalem man who had been so kind to them long ago. He greeted his guests with sorrowful countenance and led Benjamin inside, leaving Ebenezer to rest beside the door.

"Do not go to Bethlehem," he brokenly said. "After you left here, it is said wise men came from the east, clad in rich garments and bearing gifts. They sought Him who is to be King of the Jews and spoke of a great star that guided them. Herod called for the chief priests and scribes and learned Christ was to be born in Bethlehem. The cunning old fox inquired of the wise men diligently what time the star appeared. He ordered the seekers who followed the star to find the child and return, so he might also worship."

He licked his lips and swallowed hard, as if the very words of his story made a great obstruction in his throat.

Benjamin seized the man's wrist. "Go on!"

"The wise men did not return but departed into their own country another way. When Herod saw they mocked him, his rage knew no bounds. Oh, how can such a thing be!" Unashamed tears coursed down leathery cheeks. "Even now he sends forth solders to slay all the children in Bethlehem and all the coasts thereof, from two years and under, according to the time the star appeared."

The man shook his head back and forth in his grief. "That which was spoken by Jeremiah the prophet will be fulfilled, with lamentation, weeping, and great mourning — Rachel, weeping for her children and unable to be comforted, for they are not. Do not go to Bethlehem. I pray."

Benjamin's legs gave way beneath him. He dropped heavily to a nearby stool. "How could Jehovah allow such a thing?" He passed a hand over his dazed head. "My wife will soon bear a child —" Nausea threatened. He overcame it and leaped to his feet. "There may still be time. Ebenezer cannot carry me rapidly enough. I must go to Bethlehem. Perhaps the soldiers have not arrived. Or it may be Joseph and Mary have hidden the child Jesus. Kind sir, have you a mount I can borrow?"

Doubt and hope blended in the other's face. "I have and you are welcome to him. Ride swiftly, my friend. May Jehovah guide you." He motioned for Benjamin to follow and ran outside. The minute man and beast got outside the gates of Jerusalem, the belated follower urged his horse into a gallop.

Despite his best efforts, Benjamin arrived too late. He knew it the instant he reached Bethlehem. Screaming and the clash of swords greeted him. His heart sank. From the volume of agonized wailing, he sensed the main slaughter was nearing an end. Benjamin saw mothers fling themselves in front of swords to protect their babies. Terrified horses ran them down as well as their children.

The relentless soldiers battered doors, entered buildings, and more screams arose. Sickened and helpless, Benjamin had all he could do to keep from retching and to control his frightened horse. No child could escape the juggernaut. Even if the Christ-child lived, he could never find Him in the chaos that spread like a tapestry before his horrified gaze. Yet he had to gain whatever knowledge he could.

When the soldiers went away, Benjamin talked with all who would listen.

"The child that was born in a manger to Mary of Nazareth. Her husband brought her during the taxing. What of them?"

Again and again he received uncomprehending stares. On the third day, he spoke with an old man with pools of sadness for eyes.

"Did you see the wise men?" he inquired.

"Yea. They came and entered a little house near my own hut. The next day no sign remained of them or their caravan."

Benjamin's hopes leaped. He felt the blood burn in his face. "The family they visited, the carpenter and his wife?"

"Strange. I do not remember seeing Joseph after that, but the soldiers came. Surely none were spared." The old man mumbled and moved on.

Benjamin turned his mount away from the picture of death he knew would haunt him forever. Hours later he and Ebenezer started home. "The Christ-child is dead," he dully told the gray donkey. He could not continue speaking. Neither did he describe the full horror to Michal and Miriam when he reached Nazareth. Eyes red-rimmed from weeping, hair matted, unshaven and filthy, he little resembled the youthful husband who had ridden away to find the Messiah. He didn't see that Michal no longer carried a child or notice the occupied cradle in the corner.

The women refrained from questioning Benjamin until he bathed and ate a little of what they set before him. Then in sparse words he told of Herod's order. He ended by repeating, "He is dead. Herod feared losing his kingdom to the One prophesied to come out of Bethlehem and rule the people."

"Is there no chance Jesus escaped? Mary and Joseph would give their lives before allowing one hair on His head to be harmed," Michal protested, heart aching for her friends as well as her husband. "If the old man didn't see them after the wise men left, perhaps the family accompanied the caravan."

"Why would they go into a foreign land?" he countered. The next moment, torment twisted his face. He clapped his hands over his ears. "I am going mad. I cannot forget the cries of the children." He shrank back and stared at the women.

Miriam took his hands in her age-worn ones. "You are not mad, Benjamin Bar-Ara. The crying comes from your son, who hungers to see you."

"My son?" He blinked, shook his head to clear it. "How — when — ?"

81

"The very day you rode away." Michal brought the blanketed form and laid it in her husband's arms. "Jehovah's gift to us, beloved. His name is Ara."

He heard the sob in her voice but fastened his gaze on the baby's brown eyes and trusting face of his mother under a thatch of curly black hair like his own. The features blurred. A surge of father-love threatened to completely undo his self-control. He buried his face in the baby's blanket. His great shoulders heaved. Far away, fathers as well as mothers wept for their children while his own nestled safe in his strong arms.

At last he raised his head. "My quest is over. The Messiah came. The people didn't know or care. Now He has gone. Yet we shall teach this little one about Him all the days we have on this earth."

Miriam rose, magnificent in her faith. "He is not dead. I feel it in here." Her scrawny hand went to her breast. "The Lord God of Israel would not have allowed Him to come for such numbered days." She glared at one, then the other. "Michal may be right. Mary and Joseph could have gone with the wise men. Who is to say how Jehovah made a way for His Son to be saved? Benjamin, take your family to Judaea. There will be no more danger. Find a quiet place, perhaps with the sheep. One day you shall find the Messiah."

"Grandmother," Michal began.

"Be still, child." She waved her away. "I am old and ready to die. First, I must give you something. Lift the large stone in front of the fireplace and bring me the little bag beneath it."

Michal gasped when a stream of golden coins poured from the bag.

"They are yours," Miriam said. "Your parents left them. I refused to dip into the bag. Use them in your search to find the Messiah, perhaps by establishing yourself in Bethlehem. You must be where you can continue to seek Him."

Fear sprang to Michal's eyes.

"No harm will come to Ara, I promise you." Her voice rang like a prophetess. She motioned them to kneel before her. "Oh God of Israel, bless these Thy children. Hear the prayers of an old woman. Help them find the Chosen One." She paused a moment, then said with her old asperity, "Darkness has long since fallen. I seek my rest."

Long into the night Michal and Benjamin talked in whispers. He adamantly refused to leave Miriam, even though she had so ordered. "There will be time," he murmured. "When she is gone, we too shall go, although I feel there is little hope Jesus and His parents escaped the scourge."

A few weeks later, Miriam called them to her bedside. With simple dignity she said, "You are a good man, my son, the one I prayed Jehovah would send to care for Michal. I bid you both farewell." A softening came to the heavily lined face and a look akin to that of Simeon and Anna, Jonas, and Ara.

Her lips parted in a smile. Gladness filled her eyes and she strained upwards then fell back. No longer would Miriam wait for Benjamin to bring news of the Messiah. The glory in her face showed that in the twinkling between life and death, she had found Him.

Several weeks passed before Benjamin could take his little family back to Judaea. The strain of all that had transpired left Michal ill and unable to travel. Many times she roused in the night, calling for Miriam. Benjamin held her close until her tears ceased. The need to care for her baby offered gradual healing. Michal found her sorrows lessened in the joy of mothering little Ara. One day she told Benjamin, "I am ready. It is not good to remain in Nazareth. Memories of Miriam lurk in every corner.

Our lives must be elsewhere, in accordance with our promise to her."

Ebenezer had grown older and more grizzled. Michal insisted that he thrilled when she mounted him, holding her little son. "Do you remember the stories Benjamin told you of the other donkey, the one who carried the mother of our Lord to Bethlehem?" Ebenezer quickened his pace and trotted down the road with a jaunty spring to his step. Michal declared it meant he understood. Now and then he turned his head toward the tiny baby hands waving in the air.

So they traveled, down the long dusty road toward another way of life. Back to keep promises. Back to take up an interrupted quest. One day shortly before they reached the spreading tree that offered rest to weary souls. Benjamin spoke. He kept his voice low, unwilling to disturb the sleeping babe. Michal had to lean close in order to catch them and Ebenezer flicked a floppy ear.

"Perhaps we are not to find the Messiah when we are young," he stated and twisted his hand in Ebenezer's rough mane. "I do not mean just us, but anyone who seeks Him." He tried to make his troubled thoughts more clear. "The shepherds who were permitted to see Him had many more years than I. So did Ara, Simeon, and Anna. Sometimes I feel this is how it will be with all. Will He only be found when we are old and ready to leave the world behind?"

Compassion filled Michal. "I do not believe that, my husband. If only the old see and recognize Him, who is left to tell the coming generations? Besides, how old is Abner and some of the other shepherds?"

Benjamin looked startled. "Abner is in the middle of life, or was when I went away. The others are a bit older."

She smiled triumphantly. "See? It is not given just to the old to behold."

"I believe you are right," he admitted. "Abner's face, the others, when they returned from Bethlehem. I can never forget them." He put his big hand over Michal's. She saw hope rise in his expressive dark eyes. "If the Christ-child has not been spared, can a man yet live and serve Him, obey His commandments, and be granted a glimpse of Him?"

"I feel close to Him each time I look at Ara. I see His handiwork in the early morning when the sun peeps over the hill and at the day's end; in changing seasons and drifting white clouds." She raised her face to the sky. "If He created all these things, and we know He did, then is He not with us? Must we see Him with our earthly eyes in order to believe, when we feel Him all around?"

"Is this, then, what they meant — all those who prophesied I would behold Him? Abner and Ara, old Jonas and Miriam?" Longing crept into his face. "Michal, I want to go home. Let us not dwell in Bethlehem, saddened with the death of children. We shall join Abner and the others on the hillsides and in the fields and make a good life for Ara. What is more fitting than his becoming a shepherd like unto his father and grandfather before Him?"

"And your dream to find the Messiah? What of that? Miriam spoke so convincingly of the babe being spared." She held her breath.

Benjamin looked across the hills with a faraway expression in his eyes. "I do not think that can be. Yet if so, will they not one day return to Jerusalem? Every year thousands of pilgrims come for the Passover. We can go each year, watch the crowds, and wait. If the Christ-child escaped, we will find Him — someday."

Michal could not accept they would ever actually see the Messiah yet to say so would cruelly destroy her husband's lingering hope. "We shall make our abode near

Bethlehem," she agreed in her musical voice. "Our son will grow and bring us much happiness." Michal sought joy through striving to bring gladness into the life of the husband who cherished her.

"You are even more beautiful than the day at the well." Benjamin's husky voice thrilled her. She knew pleasant words did not come easy to him. Most often, his dark searching eyes showed the love he found difficult to utter.

"Our needs are simple," Michal told him. "A warm cottage and food. Let us put away Miriam's — nay — our gold coins. One day Ara may need them."

He nodded and the journey continued. When they reached the hill above Jerusalem, he said, "It is just a little later in the day than when I first saw the temple. Close your eyes, beloved." A little farther on he whispered, "Behold."

Michal opened her eyes. She stared in wonder, unprepared by all the stories of those who had seen it. The temple gleamed in the sunlight, promising all things to the faithful. She slipped from Ebenezer's back, handed Ara to Benjamin, and fell to her knees in the dusty road. "The Lord God of Israel be praised. Today I have seen His dwelling place!" Even with all the human frailty she knew accompanied the edifice, Michal felt the reverence the temple of the Most High invoked within all followers who worshiped the One God. They watched until the last sliver of light faded, leaving the temple cold and remote.

In spite of its magnificence, Michal had no desire to linger. After a night's lodging, they journeyed on. "We will stop and see Jonas, who once saved my life," Benjamin told her. He turned aside and found the hut. To their disappointment, it held no sign of habitation. Dust lay thick on the little table, the door sagged. The kind old man and his wife could not have lived there in weeks or months. Had they died, or gone elsewhere? When Benjamin did not return, had they tried to find the Messiah for themselves? Unfit for occupancy, the hut offered no welcome.

The closer they came to the fields of his childhood, the more Benjamin's face shone. Michal feared for his reception. All these months grown into years seemed a lifetime. What if Abner and the others had also disappeared? She silently scolded herself for her doubts. Benjamin had his carpentry skills and surely Abner would have left word if he left. Half the sheep belonged to Benjamin. Still, Michal plaited her fingers so tightly they whitened, aching for her husband's possible disappointment.

They topped the hill where Benjamin had once flung, "I'm coming!" to the heavens above him. Things had not turned out as expected. Yet God had been good. Michal tightened her hold on their son.

Benjamin threw back his head. His mighty lungs bellowed out the emotion Michal knew could be uttered no other way. "Abner!" Her eyes opened wide. *Abner, Abner, Abner* sang the hills. She had never been to a place that echoed a cry. Before the last note died, a man large in stature, with shaggy hair, beard, and eyebrows left the valley below and started up the hill they descended. Other shepherds joined him, meeting the travelers halfway.

"Benjamin, my son, you are a man!" Abner embraced him. The others crowded close. Abner looked at Michal and she had the feeling she could trust him with her life.

"My wife, Michal. Our son, Ara." He gently laid the baby in Abner's arms, arms that had cuddled many a motherless lamb. A tiny fist fought free of its coverings and buried itself in Abner's beard. The baby smiled.

A loud whoop of laughter swept over the

reunited band. "Welcome home," the shepherds cried.

But Abner asked, "You found the Messiah?"

"Nay. I fear He is dead at the hands of Herod. Joseph and his family were seen a few days before the soldiers came. Miriam, who cared for Michal since babyhood, believed the Christ-child lives, but it is impossible."

Abner raised his head. Something of the look on Miriam's face rested on his weather-beaten features, validating the meaning of his name — light. "I also believe He lives. I know not where or how, just that He lives."

"It cannot be." Sweat poured from Benjamin's forehead. "You were not there. No child could escape the carnage."

Abner's gaze remained fixed on Benjamin. Michal felt the world halted. Then Abner spoke. "Nay, I was not there that terrible day, but you were not there that wonderful night. When I tried to tell you about it, words vanished in the air. I beheld the babe and knew much in life could not be understood. Now I should be weeping with anguish. I cannot. I know He lives."

"If only I could believe that!" Benjamin's face worked.

Michal recognized this was a long speech

for Abner. Could it be true? Did the faithful who had once seen Him know He lived in spite of evidence to the contrary? Longing to believe for Benjamin's sake as well as her own, she said, "Perhaps the Lord God did protect Him." Hope stirred folded wings.

"He would see that His Son was spared." Abner's pronouncement sent echoes ringing throughout the valley with a hundred voices, *spared, spared, spared.* Some of the other shepherds nodded agreement. Michal realized they must be those who had traveled to Bethlehem and seen the Christ-child.

"Once you have seen Him, you will never believe Him dead," Abner said. "All you can remember is life." Michal felt the words burn into her soul. She saw in her husband's eyes they had done the same with him. One day would they come back in an hour of need to bless the hearers?

"Come, we will make a feast." Abner's mood changed. He led them to his rude lodgings not far from the fields. "It's the best I have. Tomorrow we prepare a better place. Now I will bring water. You must rid yourself of the dust of the road and rest. Then we will make merry. Have we not been blessed this day by your return?" Michal felt his gaze rest on her, then Ara, before he beamed and added, "Ah, how blessed indeed."

Evening brought no more time for serious things. Music and laughter prevailed. Benjamin whispered that Michal's beautiful face and Ara's small helplessness had captured his rough companions' hearts.

"There is need for carpenters," Abner said when Benjamin told them he planned to return to the fields. "Build yourself a home and others will seek you out. There are also always chairs, tables, and benches to be repaired. Leave the sheep to me and to Ara when he is older."

Benjamin followed Abner's advice and prospered. Every morning he and Michal faced the rising sun and gave thanks, especially after tiny Miriam came. Proud Abner continued strong and true, encouraging them with thoughts and hopes of the Messiah long after their own hopes of finding Jesus sank lower with each setting sun.

six

One by one, the years passed. Each year the little family, usually accompanied by Abner, left their home and went up with the children to the feast of the Passover in Jerusalem. Much preparation was required, for the herbs, the unleavened bread, the paschal lamb must all be in readiness for the time of remembrance.

Every year, Benjamin spent hours scanning the crowd, watching for a face he had never seen. The Christ-child would now be a young lad, sturdy like his own Ara and Miriam. What mattered the years gone into the corridors of the dusty past? There could be no question as to recognition. Benjamin would know the Son of God as surely as a lamb knew which ewe had birthed it.

Each year brought new contentment, except for the restless hunger to find his Master that gnawed inside Benjamin. Old

Ebenezer no longer worked. He dreamed in the sun when he was not following the boy Ara and his sister Miriam. Both adored him and never tired of petting their faithful friend. They also talked to him, pouring out whatever lay in their young hearts, just as their father had done since childhood.

Ara and Miriam. Even the sound of their names brought joy to their parents' hearts. The attending physician when Miriam came into the world had shaken his head and warned there would be no more children. Michal and Benjamin gave the love that would have been divided among many to the two children whose laughter brought answering smiles from all who knew them.

In the tenth year after the belated follower came back to the Bethlehem area with his bride, Benjamin sadly looked at Abner and Michal. "I cannot go to Jerusalem." He touched his right leg and winced. A sharp tool had slipped, leaving a deep gash in the leg. Although Michal bound it tightly, using ointment made of herbs, much pain persisted. Benjamin could not stand on it for long.

"You must look for the Christ-child." Benjamin shook his head. "I know not why I tell you this. It has been too many years. Surely if He escaped Herod's slaughter some word would have come to us."

Despondent from the wound that prevented him from working, he found it hard to watch the others make ready for the journey.

"I will stay with you, my husband." Trouble rested in Michal's clear brown eyes. Time had been kind to her. Not a single thread of silver marred the rich dark brown of her hair. The flesh of her oval face remained firm and soft. Her lips curved upwards with the peace that comes from loving and being loved.

"Nay. I would not have it so," Benjamin hastily said. He regretted he had allowed his feelings to spoil her pleasure. "Ara is ten, Miriam six. They can care for me well, if they will?"

He saw the struggle in Ara's eyes before he said, "Of course we will, Father." Miriam nodded. They watched the little caravan until it disappeared from sight, then turned to stroke Ebenezer's shaggy coat. The donkey brayed with delight.

Benjamin sank to a bench of his own making just inside the open door and listened to his children's chatter. A smile crossed his grave face. His dark eyes gleamed beneath the still-curly mop of black hair. How could he mourn when God had given him Miriam, a miniature Michal; and Ara, tall and capable.

"Tell me the story of the baby," Miriam demanded, small hands entwined in Ebenezer's mane.

Ara, with his advanced age and wisdom, crossed his arms over his tunic-clad chest. "A little donkey like Ebenezer carried Mary to Bethlehem. No one had room for her and Joseph, so Jesus had to be born in a stable. His mother laid Him in a manger." Awe filled the eyes turned toward the sky. "An angel came to the fields and told Father and Abner and all the other shepherds. They were afraid, but the angel said to fear not. Other angels sang." His eyes glistened. "They went away. Grandfather Ara, whose name I bear, and the others went to Bethlehem and saw the Christ-child. All but Father. He stayed with the sheep."

"If you had been Father, would you have stayed behind?"

A manly look came to the lad's face. "Did we not stay with Father? I would if the sheep needed me, but oh, I would be sorry I could not go see the Messiah!"

A pang went through Benjamin. The price of faithfulness had been high. If he were again faced with the choice . . . He pushed the thought aside.

"What is a messiah?" Miriam asked, as she asked each time Ara told her the story they loved and had heard a dozen, nay, a hundred times.

"Someone who will take care of His people, as Abner and I take care of the sheep. He will be our leader and the soldiers will never again kill children like us. Someday He will come and be our King."

Many expressions flitted over Miriam's innocent face. "What will He do with the Roman soldiers?"

Had not Benjamin asked the same question again and again? He held his breath, wondering how Ara would answer.

"I do not know, my sister. I do know He will do what is right." Assurance rang in Ara's treble tones.

"Then we need not worry." Miriam freed her hands from Ebenezer's mane and clapped them. "Come. We will gather flowers for Father." They ran through the fields, stopping now and then to roll in the grass and chase golden butterflies.

How easily weighty matters are forgotten in the simple joy of being alive, Benjamin thought. For a moment, he wished he could be a child once more, free of care. He slowly shook his head. Nay. 'Twas no fair exchange. He raised his face to the sky, even as his son had done. "Lord, my life will be complete if I may gaze on the face of Thy Son before I die. Grant me this blessing, I pray."

Not long after, in Jerusalem, Michal hummed and carefully extinguished the last embers of her breakfast fire. She watched the separated embers turn gray and die. If only Benjamin and the children could have come. How they enjoyed camping on the hillsides, along with hundreds of other pilgrims to the Passover. Only the wealthy could afford the exorbitant rates asked for even the meanest accommodations. Abner and the shepherds — some with wives and children — looked after her well, but Michal missed her family. A small smile curved her sweet lips. Passover had ended. Within the hour they would start home.

Anticipation lent a lovely rose to her smooth cheeks. The God of Israel had given her great blessings. Grant she might be worthy of them. A prayer first uttered by David rose to her lips. "Let the words of my mouth, and the meditation of my heart, be acceptable in Thy sight, O Lord, my strength, and my redeemer."

As if thought of Abner had conjured him up, he strode toward her, a strange look on his face, one she had never before seen him wear.

"What is it? Surely no harm has come to our loved ones." Michal clutched his rough sleeve with frantic fingers.

"Nay." He smiled but excitement brightened his face above his beard. "Michal, something causes me to believe I should not yet return with you. I know not what this feeling of urgency is, but I cannot leave Jerusalem so long as it is in my heart to stay."

"Does it concern — the Messiah?" Her heart pounded.

He shook his head. "I cannot say. I only know I must tarry for a time. You will be well cared for on the journey home and I will come soon.

Something fluttered inside Michal and warred with her desire for home and family. It caused her to say. "Perhaps I, too, should abide."

"Nay. Gossip-mongers would accuse you of sin for remaining when the other women go, even though my years are nearly twice those of your own." The corners of his mouth turned down.

So it was arranged and Abner stayed in Jerusalem. Three days passed uneventfully. Still he lingered, unable to explain why. "Tomorrow I go," he muttered. Restlessness drove him to the temple, where a crowd had gathered. "What is it?"

"A young lad, not more than twelve years. See? He dares question the learned doctors. Has ever such a thing occurred in the history of the world?"

Abner's heart thumped. He forced his way to where he could see and blood beat in his temples. *Twelve years old? Disputing the doctors? Could it be —* ? Abner could only get a quick glimpse of the daring lad. It proved disappointing. From the back, at least, he neither looked nor dressed differently than any other child his age. The next moment Abner gasped. The things he said — why, they were far beyond anything one his age could know, even if he had studied the law of Moses since birth!

Abner felt his mouth go dry, his body tremble. He slipped closer, saw the amazement on the learned men's faces at the boy's answers and understanding.

A slight commotion to one side whipped Abner around. A tall man and slight woman, evidently his wife, came to the boy. Their faces showed disturbance.

"We supposed thee to be in the company going home," the man said. His kind, dark eyes showed lingering concern. When we could not find thee after a day's journey, we sought thee among kinfolk and acquaintances. When we still found thee not, we returned to Jerusalem seeking our son. We have worried so! Now, after three days, we find thee in the temple in the midst of the doctors, both hearing them and asking them questions."

The woman spoke. "Son, why hast thou thus dealt with us? Behold, thy father and I have sought thee sorrowing."

The voice sounded familiar, but the woman's hood kept Abner from seeing her face. His brow wrinkled. He peered more closely but failed to identify her.

A clear voice like the tones of a finely crafted bell replied, "How is it that ye sought me? Wist ye not that I must be about my Father's business?"

Abner pulled at his beard. What did the lad mean? He had no chance to find out for father, mother, and boy slipped out. A multitude swept between them and the shepherd. He fought his way through, but when he reached the street, no trace of them remained.

"Why do I feel the same way I did that night long ago?" Abner whispered. "As if I stood on holy ground?" He shrugged. "The lad has wisdom beyond his years, 'tis true. Yet the parents are simple folk. Their garb shows that."

Simple folk. His eyes widened. Had not Joseph, the carpenter and Mary, his wife been the same? With a loud cry that drew unwelcome attention from those who thronged by, Abner rushed from person to person. "Did you see them? A tall man. A woman. A lad about twelve?"

Scowls and blank faces greeted him. No one knew or cared who they were or where they had gone. After searching for two full days with no success, Abner turned his face toward Bethlehem. His heart, a heavy stone, ached. How could he tell Benjamin? The question perched on his shoulder all the way home.

In the cool twilight evening, Abner told his story. He writhed at the pain in his friend's face, the open-mouthed stares of the others. "I don't know that it was Jesus," he cried.

"Nay." Benjamin's voice sounded lifeless.

"I did learn something," Abner mumbled. "Vague rumors are abroad in Jerusalem that a single child escaped Herod's order of death."

"What!" Benjamin's body jerked as if struck.

"It is said in whispers, that the night before the slayings a certain man fled with his family, leaving a deserted house and most of their possessions."

"Where did they go?" Benjamin burst out.

Abner shook his graying head. "No one knows for sure, but the whisperers say an angel appeared to Joseph in a dream. It is reported the angel warned him to take the young child and his mother to Egypt and stay until further word came to them; that Herod sought to destroy their son. The family supposedly left in the darkest night hours, carrying only those things they could hastily pack."

"It would account for the fact no one knew where they had gone or when," Benjamin said hoarsely. He stared at Michal. Her eyes reflected newborn hope.

Abner brokenly said, "Forgive me. You sent me to find the Christ-child. I failed, when it may have been He whose voice I heard in the temple, whose face I glimpsed." He bowed his massive head, suffering etched in every valley of his lined face.

Ara and Miriam ran to him, awkwardly patting the heaving shoulders. "Abner, it is enough that He lives, is it not?" Ara demanded.

A convulsion went through the man. He raised his head and stared at the boy.

"He has spoken well." Benjamin limped

to his friend and embraced him. "We must not regret what is past. Good friend, I know what it is to be too late." His face twisted in remembered agony, made fresh by the conviction the lad in the temple really had been Jesus. Yet even as he comforted Abner, his tortured mind cried, *O, Lord, how long? Will it always be so? Must there always be one hill between, one more bend in the road? Will my entire life be one of missing Thee? One of trailing a few steps behind when I long to walk beside Thee? Son of David, have mercy on me.*

He wondered that the words did not tear from his throat. Yet in the face of Abner's great loss, he could not voice them. Michal's eyes showed she understood, then and in the days that followed. Always he wondered. Should he rise and go to Jerusalem? What could he find out, when Abner had been able to learn so little? The Messiah was moving farther away all the time. Benjamin warily stretched the muscles of his right leg. Searing pain sent great drops of sweat to his brow. He could not travel, at least for a time.

One night he dreamed. He stood in the fields of his youth, keeping watch over the sheep. The great light of long ago came again along with the message, praising God and bringing peace and good will to earth.

He felt himself calmed, healed. He awakened to early dawn. The sun had no more than suggested its arrival by a rosy glow in the east. Michal lay sleeping beside him, dark hair undone from her night plait and tumbling to her shoulders.

The sun burst over the hill and flooded the room with its glory. Benjamin's spirits rose to meet it. As long as the sun came up each day, hope remained — to overcome the dark night fears and offer promise only a new day can bring.

He had need of the memory. Without it, he would have packed away his dream of finding the Messiah. His leg healed and he went to Jerusalem but came home disheartened. As Abner had reported, no one knew or cared about one humble family among the hordes of those who came to Passover.

Weeks became months. Months turned to years. Even as Benjamin had foreseen, those who beheld the angels told the story with such unshaken belief, their children and grandchildren believed and marveled. Time took its inevitable toll. Ebenezer lay down one evening and refused to get up. The children cried and ran to their parents for comfort. Dear old Abner, whose dim eyes yet glowed with the same deep fire as in his youth, went to join Ara and receive his reward. His last words prophesied Benjamin would yet find the Christ.

Miriam and young Ara grew tall and comely. Both married children with whom they once played, now grown to young men and women. They, in turn, had children of their own.

Benjamin continued strong, but the years at last brought frailty to Michal. Although in her husband's eyes she remained the same lovely girl he first met at the well in Nazareth, even he noticed the wracking cough and the way she tired so easily.

One evening they walked the fields together. "He would be thirty now," Benjamin said. All the longing of years blended in his voice.

"Yea." She pressed her head against his shoulder. "Do you still think we shall find Him?"

He noticed how she said "we" and rejoiced that his dream had become her own. "I do not know, but my dreams are troubled. I see the Christ-child. Then I see a tall figure in the midst of confusion. I wait with a feeling of loss, as if something precious has been taken. I awaken before it is revealed to me and I fear. Sometimes things to come cast their shadow."

Michal sighed, and he roused to gather her up in strong arms and bear her back to their home.

One afternoon a neighboring shepherd stopped by. "Have you heard the news?" His eyes burned. "One has come preaching in the wilderness of Judaea. He wears garments of camel's hair and eats locusts and wild honey. He thunders for men to repent of their sins, and says the kingdom of heaven is at hand." He stopped to gulp the cool drink Michal hastily offered him and rushed on. "He stands in the Jordan River and baptizes all who will hear and believe!"

"Is he the Messiah?" Benjamin's sinews tightened and his chest hurt.

"Nay, he is called John. He says he is the voice of one who cries in the wilderness, saying, 'Prepare ye the way of the Lord, make His paths straight.' He also says One will come after him so much mightier that he is not worthy to bear that One's shoes! He tells those who listen he baptizes with water, but the One to come will baptize with the Holy Ghost and with fire."

The messenger drank more. "I myself allowed him to bury me in the water and never have I felt so free." He put down the emptied vessel from which he drank. "Benjamin, go and see for yourself. This John is mighty and unlike anyone we have ever known."

"Does he baptize women as well as men?" Michal pressed a hand to her lips.

"Oh, yes! All who come and are willing. I must go now and tell others." He sprang up and left with only a hasty, "Peace unto you" to serve as farewell.

Before Benjamin would consent to their seeking John, he made inquiry about the new preacher. He learned he had stirred up a great deal of interest. Crowds flocked to hear him and he baptized hundreds. John excluded no one from the need to repent. He enraged Herod with his scorn and publicly denounced Herod for taking his brother Philip's wife, Herodias, to his bed. He told the Pharisees and Sadducees they were a generation of vipers and needed repentance as much as anyone else.

At last Benjamin and Michal sought John the Baptizer. Nay, he was not the Messiah, yet power and truth flowed from his bearded lips, holiness from his piercing eyes. A quick glance between husband and wife showed them in agreement. They stood among the others and waited for the rite called *baptism*. Into the depths John laid them. Benjamin knew they emerged new creatures.

An old man with shining face stood near when they stepped to one side. "I have seen the hope of my generation. I saw Him. They say He is the baptizer's cousin, Jesus, son of Joseph the carpenter of Nazareth."

"Jesus?" Benjamin felt the blood drain from his face.

"Yea. He came to be baptized with the rest of us." Glory rested in the seamed face. "John told Him he had need to be baptized of Him!"

"What did Jesus say?" Benjamin choked out the words.

"Something about needing to fulfill all righteousness. But that was not all. When he rose from the water, a dove lighted on his shoulder, as if the heavens had opened and allowed it to float down. I thought I heard a voice." The man broke off. Sudden fear shone in his aged eyes and he shrank back. His gaze darted from side to side like one seeking a way to escape the consequences of his folly in talking so freely to strangers.

"Wait!" Benjamin laid a detaining hand on the other's shaking arm. "You have nothing to fear from us. Tell us what he said, this Jesus."

seven

"What did the voice say?" Benjamin repeated. He shook the man's scrawny arm. "No harm shall come to you from telling us. We long with all our hearts to find the Chosen One."

"I am not sure, but I thought I heard the words, 'This is my beloved son, in whom I am well pleased.'" The old man pulled away as if regretting he had spoken and vanished into the crowd.

"Can it be Jesus?" Michal exclaimed. "Cousin of the baptizer?"

"I must follow and question," Benjamin told her. Yet the crowd had swallowed the informer. Many old men with faces averted moved among the multitude. Searching for one resembled seeking a single grain of sand on the shores of the Jordan where John continued to baptize.

A long while later, Benjamin returned to

Michal. They slowly separated themselves from the throng, traveled home, and again grew absorbed in their lives, only with a difference. Hope that had lain like a tightly folded bud unfurled anew.

Snatches of rumor came, disturbing their newfound peace. Herodias had been so furious at the wild man who dared say she sinned, she turned her full wrath toward him. Before long, John lay in prison. Could Benjamin and Michal use the long-hoarded gold pieces to buy his freedom? Nay. What need had Herodias of their paltry sum, magnificent as it appeared in their eyes. No ransom would satisfy the wicked heart that beat inside her pampered body.

Other rumors proved equally upsetting. Gossip had it Jesus had vanished — perhaps to Galilee or Nazareth or Capernaum. Some said He entered the desert and remained for forty days and nights. It was also noised abroad He had recruited an unruly band of men He called disciples, as motley a bunch as could be assembled. They ranged from a hated tax gatherer to rough fishermen.

"Strange companions for a Messiah, if He is one," Benjamin told Michal. She looked as troubled as he felt.

Not for all the gold of Rome would she tell her husband how troubled she really was. Michal had used up most of her strength in seeking John. Before beginning the journey, she had fervently prayed for healing. If only she could have risen from her infirmities when she rose from the waters of the Jordan!

It had not happened that way. Although she felt cleansed inside and out, the cough and weakness persisted. Night after night, while her husband lay sleeping at her side, silent drops slid from beneath her tightly closed eyelids. A long ago memory haunted her, the conversation she and Benjamin had shared at the time he asked her to become his wife.

Think you I would ever stand in the way of your keeping your promise to your God? Oh, Benjamin, how little you know me!

His stubborn voice. *It would not be fair. Suppose we became as one and I learned where I could find the Messiah? What then? Already I have missed Him not one, but two times. Yet how could I leave you?*

Then her own voice, strong and unafraid. *Benjamin Bar-Ara, what matter it how long you took? One day you would return and find me waiting. . . .*

Michal shuddered. Benjamin had become her heart, her life. Never in the history of the world had any woman felt more loved, more cherished than she. From him she took her strength. If she released him to seek the Messiah, would she even be alive when he returned? Her chest grew constricted with the weight of what lay ahead. "I cannot let him go," she whispered into the hand that tightly covered her mouth.

You cannot let him stay, a warning voice whispered in her mind.

Too weak to continue fighting, Michal lay rigid. She longed to rise but forced herself to relax. Benjamin had grown attuned to her slightest movement in the night. He needed his rest. She saw daily the struggle in his heart, the war that pulled him between his wife and his long delayed quest.

"Lord, I pray for the courage to let go, no matter the cost," she brokenly whispered. "Grant me Thy strength, for I have little of my own and cannot overcome my weakness without Thy help." A short while later, Michal slept the first real sleep she had enjoyed in all the time since they heard of the baptizer's cousin Jesus.

Early the next morning, Michal donned her simple robe and a mantle of faith. When the first meal of the day ended, she told Benjamin, "It is time for you to go. We must know if this Jesus is the Christ-child born so long ago in Bethlehem."

She saw gladness leap to her husband's eyes. Sadness quickly replaced it. He shook his head. "I cannot go just yet." He did not say why, but she knew only too well.

"You must," she insisted. "I am feeling stronger this day. Ara and his wife are nearby, as are Miriam and her husband. I shall not be lonely nor neglected. Jehovah will protect me. Beloved, go, for my sake, as well as your own." She felt renewed urgency even as she spoke. "Do you not see? We must know if He is the One."

Benjamin jerked as if stung by arrows. His face brightened, the way the hillsides near Bethlehem did when first touched by the slow-rising sun. "Are you sure, my Michal?" Some of the light fled from his strong features. "Perhaps I am too old. I have failed to find Him so many times. Can I risk trying again, only to discover this Jesus is not the Promised One?" His mighty fist crashed to the table, but his voice dropped to such a low pitch, Michal had to bend near to hear him. "I-I do not think I can bear to fail again."

His deep and burning gaze fastened on her, but she knew his thoughts ran far from their home. "Great multitudes have begun to follow this Jesus who surrounds Himself with the offscouring of the earth. Surely a

King would companion with a better class of people."

"Did you not think long ago surely angels would appear to the noble and wise, not to humble shepherds?" A core of strength she knew must be in answer to her prayers began to form in Michal's heart. "All these years, you have declared once you see the Deliverer's face, you will know Him. Nothing must keep you from finding out for yourself if this Jesus is who men say He is."

A short bark of laughter held no mirth. Benjamin's lips firmed. "According to the chief priests and scribes, He is a blasphemer and a fraud. Others say He is a good man. Still others feel He is deluded. Perhaps He is. Perhaps the Son of God perished in Herod's butchery." He rose in such haste, the couch on which he sat overturned. "I must think on it." He strode out, leaving Michal defeated and wondering if ever again she would be brave enough to broach the subject uppermost in her mind — and his.

The moon waxed and waned, again and again. Still Benjamin tarried. He hesitated too long. By the time he realized he must find this Jesus, Michal had faded into a wilted flower. He could not, would not, leave her, despite the pleading in her eyes.

116

They looked too large in her thin face with its transparent skin. Often he wondered if her strange illness no physician had yet diagnosed had fallen on her because her husband had forsaken his quest. Was he to blame?

One night when she fell into a restless sleep, Benjamin slipped away and sought the solace of the fields outside the house. Gazing into the star-dotted heavens he knew so well, remorse all but consumed him. Why had he not gone when he could, all those months ago when Michal urged him? What kind of God visited plagues on an innocent woman because of her husband's unpaid vow? Despair swept through him like a keen wind in winter. So did his feeling of insignificance. What was Benjamin Bar-Ara next to the countless stars? A mere man. A single speck of dust. He shivered and drew his robe close, but it warmed him not. Unable to stand the feelings never before present in his heart, he fell to the earth, bowed low and cried, "Why, Lord?"

No answer came. After a time he slept from sheer exhaustion. He roused to a strange light and rubbed his eyes. Was he dreaming? Nay. Leaves rustled nearby. Was it a vision? He did not know. All he knew was that a luminous, shining figure stood before him. Not an angel, such as the one who once brought fear, then peace. This was the figure of a man, face partly hidden by a shadow.

Deep, dark eyes glowed with compassion. Benjamin saw little else. Once he looked into the Master's eyes, nothing mattered. Now he understood Ara, Abner, others who vowed they had nothing to live for once they saw the Messiah.

Benjamin longed to cry out but could utter no sound until the Presence smiled. He held out a shaking hand, longing to know if what he saw was real. The figure did not move, yet Benjamin's fingers fell short. The iron bands holding his tongue loosed. "Is it really You? I have missed You so many times. When I could have followed, I feared. Now Michal is ill, unto death, I fear. How can I stay when I have promised to follow? How can I go when she needs me so?" More than thirty years of longing made the question a poignant cry. "What shall I do?"

The radiant figure dimmed, although Benjamin had no sense the Christ had moved. He desperately cried out again, feeling he could not let this only chance pass by. "Tell me. What shall I do?"

Was it only the wind, or did the single word "tarry" hover, a feather in the air?

Benjamin felt peace drop over him like a sheepskin cloak. The glow lessened and he called, "Will I ever find You again?"

Again he knew not whether the reply existed only in his mind, yet the word "someday" sank into him and glowed like a rare gem in the light of a setting sun. The misty figure disappeared completely, leaving Benjamin alone. He longed to rush and tell Michal, but something held him. Drained, yet exalted, he watched the stars go out one by one. Not until dawn came and heavy dew settled on the land did he rouse to a low call.

"Benjamin, where are you?"

Contrition smote him. Sandals wet from the dew, he entered the house.

Michal gasped. "Your face. Why, you look no older than the day we met at the well. What has happened to bring the fire back to your eyes?"

He knelt beside the bed. "I have seen the Master. He came to me. Dream or vision, I know not. Michal, I am to tarry, not follow. Someday I will find Him again. I felt His unspoken promise in my heart. It is enough."

He saw relief in Michal's eyes and knew she felt reprieved. He wanted to snatch her to his bosom and hold her close to the heart that proclaimed with every beat, *you have found Him.* Instead, he buried his face in her dark hair and wept like a child. His rough hand stroked Michal's wet face in a moment made holy by their joy.

Weeks later, saddened by the loss of Ara's wife and the son who breathed but once before joining his mother in death, Benjamin asked Michal, "Long ago my father knew he could not follow the Chosen One. He asked me to go in his stead. Do you think Ara would take up the search? His crops are in. Miriam and her husband will care for his other children. I long to know if Jesus is indeed the Messiah who came to me in the fields."

Michal's eyes shone. "Ara, the lion! How fitting, that the grandson of one who desired with all his heart to seek should do so. I believe Ara will consent."

At close of day, Benjamin again told the story of his quest and ended with the visitation in the fields, if indeed it had been one. He looked deep into the eyes and face that reflected the young man he had once been. Nay, a combination of that man and his strong father. "My son, will you go?"

"I will be honored." The husky voice betrayed humility rather than pride at being chosen. "Mother, it is said this Jesus raises sick ones from their beds of affliction. As soon as I find Him, I will send word. Surely He will heal you if you come." He clasped her wasted hands.

"It shall be as the Lord wills, my son."

He stood and stretched to full height. In the prime of manhood, he appeared invincible. If anyone could travel the long road to find the Messiah, surely that one was Ara. Benjamin's heart beat strong within him at the thought.

"My son, take these." Michal pressed hard, gold coins in his hand.

"Nay, I have no need of them. I have saved enough to carry me for many months, although God willing, it will not take so long."

"I pray it will be so," she whispered, then laid her frail hand on her son's head in blessing. Benjamin did the same. A mist rose in three pairs of eyes when the petitions for a safe and successful journey ended.

Dawn barely streaked the sky when Ara slipped away the next morning. Farewells had been said the night before. He secretly wondered if his mother would live until he found Jesus. Even if she did, would her weakness permit her to travel? He pushed aside the brooding thoughts and mounted his strong horse Zerah, named for the dawn. "No shaggy gray Ebenezer on this journey," he told the black when they rode away, carrying only what they would require.

Ara paused at the top of the hill and looked back with sadness and anticipation. How many endless miles stretched between him and Jesus? How long would it be before he and Zerah again stood in this spot?

A figure appeared in the doorway of the house below: Benjamin, standing with upraised hand. Ara knew his father would travel with him in spirit. Was Benjamin not sending part of himself? The thought flowed over Ara like honey in the sun. He lifted a hand, wheeled Zerah, and started down the dusty road, seeking the One who at some time in their lives calls all men.

Ara carried no jewels or fine ointments, yet he bore great treasure: the hopes and dreams of more than thirty years. The knowledge made him pause part way down the side of the first hill, out of sight of the keen gaze he felt still remained fixed on the other side of the hillside. He must find the Messiah. If Jesus were not the One, he would go on — no matter how long it took or at what cost.

"God of Abraham, Isaac, and Jacob, hear

Thy child's cry. Go with me, I pray." Ara guided Zerah away from a clump of grass and urged him ahead. Then he threw his head back in the same powerful response to the call of the Master his father and grandfather before him had shouted to the sky, "I am coming!"

"Will Ara never return?" Michal restlessly turned on her bed. The sound of her voice sounded loud and rang in the corners of the empty room. In all the weeks and months of her son's absence, never had she let her loneliness show. How she missed the manchild, given to her as a gift from on high! Before Benjamin, Miriam, and the others, she kept a cheerful countenance and hid her pain. She outwardly agreed it might take Ara a long time but eagerly awaited news — at first. Messages sent by various means were sometimes lost or mislaid. Yet Michal clung to the hope they would hear soon.

When they did, then what? Could Jesus rebuke the illness within her and set her free? Or would freedom only come with death? She feared it not, but grief at having to leave those she loved haunted her. A thought forced itself into her reluctant mind. Did the Holy One of Israel know only Michal's death could free Benjamin to seek

Him? Could she make the sacrifice necessary, should it be so? The sunlit room filled with the intensity of her thoughts.

Determination came and a surge of relinquishment. "I, too, have prayed to see Thee. Let it be done unto me according to Thy will. If Thou chooses not to spare me, still will I trust Thee, unto death and beyond." It took every ounce of strength she possessed to turn herself wholly into God's keeping. Why did the words sound familiar?

Spent, she returned in memory to the days in Nazareth and realized Mary had offered such a prayer. Where was her friend now, the virgin who had been chosen as a vessel for God's own Son? Did she travel with Him? Joseph had been much older than Mary. Perhaps he was dead.

Strangely calm, Michal slept. She awakened refreshed, more so than she had been in months. In a few days her pain receded. Color returned to her face. She called for bread and meat to replace the broth that had been all she could get down for many weeks.

Benjamin summoned the finest physician in Bethlehem. He described Michal's improvement before the man went to the invalid. "I dare not believe she will be well, yet this very day she got from her bed and began directing the ways of the household.

What do you make of it?"

"I cannot say without seeing her." The physician stroked his beard. "However, at times there is a final rallying before death." He brushed past Benjamin, after bidding him to remain where he stood.

The physician silently conducted his examination. Michal smiled to herself, well knowing what he would find. Nay, what he would not find.

"Sir, come in." The physician threw wide the door and ushered Benjamin inside. He turned to Michal. "Woman, what have you done?" Great drops of sweat stood on his forehead.

"Why do you ask?" She smiled again, hugging her arms to her breast.

He passed a hand over his dazed eyes. "I find no cough and little trace of illness. If you keep on like this for a few more weeks, I see no reason you should ever again be troubled. I ask you again, what have you done?"

A broken gasp came from Benjamin. Michal saw glory in his face. It brought the tears she had held back even in her moment of surrender. Her lips trembled. "I told Jehovah if He wanted to take me, it was all right; I submitted myself completely to His will."

"Y-you accepted death if it be wh-what Jehovah asked?" the disbelieving physician stuttered.

"And found life." She rose and walked straight into her husband's arms.

"In all my days, truly have I not seen or heard of such a thing," the physician exclaimed. He gathered the tools of his trade and departed, still mumbling to himself.

Michal scarcely saw him go. "I am well, Benjamin." She saw the struggle to believe in his dark eyes that looked down on her. She felt it in the arms that held her and heard it in the unsteady voice that asked, "Heart of my heart, are you sure?"

Love for him surged through her. She gazed at him with glowing brown eyes. She clasped both hands around his neck and pulled him close. "As sure as my knowledge of God's mercy and my husband's love."

With a low cry, he kissed the cheeks beginning to grow round, the white forehead, the upturned lips. For a long, long time they spoke no more.

A few days later a message arrived from Ara.

Peace be with you. So much has happened. I could write for hours and still not tell you all I have seen. First I must tell you:

although I have not yet caught up with the man Jesus, I am convinced He must be the One we have sought for so long, the Chosen One, the Messiah.

"Praise be to the living God!" Benjamin shouted.

Michal could not speak, so great was her joy. How much they had been given, the belated follower and his family. If they were to serve Him all the days of their lives, they could never return to God even a small portion of what He had done for them.

eight

Benjamin's voice cracked when he returned to reading the epistle. So vividly did Ara write, Michal felt she rode with him and experienced all he had.

You will remember when I left we knew not where I should start looking. Jehovah blessed me. I soon joined a group of those who longed to find Jesus as much as I did. We traveled into Galilee and came to a small village called Cana. Mother, Father, how can I tell you what I heard? Words are such poor tools to express the excitement that yet abounds from an incident that occurred a few weeks before we arrived. I will write exactly as it was told me by one of the village's finest citizens, known for his devotion to truth.

A marriage feast had been prepared. Jesus, His mother Mary, and those men He has called as disciples and who follow Him everywhere came. Far more guests than expected caused the wine supply to give out in the midst of the celebration. The bride and groom knew great shame, not enough provision had been made for those who came to wish them well.

You will find what happened hard to believe. I did. Yet my informant swore by all things in heaven and earth below he related nothing save the truth. Mary told Jesus there was no more wine. He ordered six stone water pots filled with water, then commanded drink be drawn and taken to the governor of the feast.

The ruler of the feast tasted it. Surprise crossed his face. He then made merry with the bridegroom for keeping the best wine back until the rest had been drunk! The man with whom I spoke reported he himself had drunk of the good wine that had been water. No one knows what to make of it — or of Jesus.

Benjamin paused again. His eyes gleamed.

Michal felt a smile spread over her face and into her heart. "How kind of Jesus not to allow the marriage day to be spoiled by lack of wine."

"Only a god or a devil could perform such a task," Benjamin commented and went back to Ara's letter.

I had to lay my writing aside for a time as we travel rapidly, trying to catch up with Jesus, who surely is somewhere on the road ahead. We went to Nazareth and learned the family came back from Egypt after Herod died. Jesus had been there recently. It will never be the same! He went into the synagogue on the Sabbath, as is the custom, and stood to read. They delivered to Him the writings of the prophet Isaiah. He read, "The Spirit of the Lord is upon me, because He hath anointed me to preach the gospel to the poor, He hath sent me to heal the brokenhearted, to preach deliverance to the captives, and recovering of sight to the blind, to set at liberty them that are bruised, to preach the acceptable year of the Lord." When He closed the book He told them scripture had been fulfilled in their ears that day.

They murmured among themselves, saying, "Is this not Joseph's son?" Jesus responded by saying no prophet is honored in his own country. They rose and thrust Him out of the city, meaning to cast Him headlong from the brow of a hill.

Michal moaned but cheered when Benjamin hurried on. "Do not grieve. Ara writes Jesus passed through their midst and went His way, although no one knows how."

"Praise to Jehovah!" she cried, knees weak with relief. "Is there more?"

"Just that Ara and the others were going to Capernaum, where Jesus was said to be." He scanned the page. A great chuckle rose from his belly and bellowed into the room. "He closes by saying he knows if you come to Jesus, you will be made well. Oh, what news we have for our son." He laughed again, face boyish with mischief and the thrill of surprising Ara.

Michal joined in her husband's enjoyment. "I did not go to Jesus, yet the spirit of Jehovah came to me. It matters not how I have been healed, only that I am well and free." She held out a shapely arm from which her loose sleeve fell back. How different from the wasted limbs of such a short time before! "Now that I am strong, we shall go to Jesus when Ara sends word where to find Him."

"Can a man really lead another to Him?" Benjamin wondered. "It must be so. Otherwise, Jesus would not have called disciples."

Michal thrilled to the thought. "Surely

Jesus and His disciples will come to Jerusalem for the Passover, which soon approaches. We shall be there. Ara will come, I am sure." She clasped her hands and anticipation shone in her face. "Benjamin, we may find Jesus even before our son does so. How I long to gaze into His eyes. I must know for myself He is truly the Messiah, not just from the witness of others, no matter how reliable they are."

"I, too." He nodded his head. Silver threads shone bright in the black curls. "As you said, Passover time comes soon. We have much to do before we go.

He laid the message of good cheer aside. "It won't be long." Rich color flowed into his face. A new sparkle crept into his eyes. "Our sacrifice in the temple this year will be one of thanksgiving and praise."

Days pelted by like a small child chasing a favorite lamb, marked with high hopes and abiding peace. Never had the family felt such a thrill about going to Jerusalem for the Passover, although every trip held the promise of adventure. Miriam, her husband, the children, Benjamin, and Michal finished their preparations and started their journey.

None showed more excitement than Timothy, Ara's son who, with his little sister

Sara, abided with Miriam in the absence of their father. His round black eyes missed nothing. He reminded Michal so much of Ara at a young age she sometimes called him by the wrong name. Timothy asked more questions than there were stars in the heavens.

"Grandmother, will my father be in Jerusalem? Is he one of Jesus' disciples now? If so, will he never come back to Sara and me? Do you think we'll see Jesus? Is He the Messiah? Are you really well and strong? Why do the Romans and their horses push past us so rudely? Are they going to find the Messiah, too? Why did Jehovah make some flowers yellow, others blue? What makes the grass green? Where will we stay in Jerusalem?"

Michal hid a smile and gave him the best answers she could. A prayer to the Most High God on the lad's behalf rose from her overflowing heart. *Grant that this, Thy child, may ever be alive to the wonder of Thy world, oh, Lord.*

A merry crowd gathered around their little fire that evening. They carefully followed every tradition for the keeping of the Passover. First came the repeating of the story of their forefathers' flight from Egypt, led by the hand of God through His servant

Moses. Even the youngest child knew the meaning of the bitter herbs to remind them of the bitter years in captivity and wandering in the wilderness and the paschal lamb, sacrificed for the sins of the people.

If only Ara were there! Michal sighed. No further word had come after the one ecstatic letter. "All must be well," she whispered to her mother's heart. "Bad news flies on eagle's wings. Good news often plods along the dusty highway."

Early the next morning, Benjamin stood before his wife. "Today I shall seek Him. Will you come?" Eagerness lifted the corners of his mouth.

Michal shook her head. "Go, my husband. If you find the Messiah, send word and I will hasten to you. For now I must stay with Miriam and the children." She glanced at Timothy, who rebelliously stood with hands on the hips of his tunic, black eyes filled with disappointment. She quickly added, "Take Timothy with you."

"Very well. Come, child." Benjamin turned and started down the incline toward the temple. Timothy trotted happily beside him, taking two steps for each of his grandfather's long strides.

"Why am I called Timothy?" he wanted to know. "Why was I not named Tobias or

Thaddeus or Thomas? What does Timothy mean?"

Benjamin chose to answer his last question first, although he didn't slacken his ground-consuming walk. "Timothy means honoring God. Your parents wished to express the gratitude they felt when they learned you would come."

He reflected for a moment, head cocked to one side like an inquisitive creature of the wild. "Is my mother with Jehovah?"

Benjamin hesitated. "I feel in my heart she is with Ara and Abner and others who have gone before. Some say death is the end. Yet the grass that dies, lives again. Is grass, then, more important than people? I think not."

A skinny hand, grubby in spite of all the washing Michal insisted on, slipped into Benjamin's. "If you say it, this must be true. You are the wisest man in the world. My father said so."

Benjamin felt a rush of emotion. He looked down at the trusting child. Words he had spoken the night the angels sang in the field returned to him. *My father never tires. This day I watched him chase a wolf from the flock. The beast fled before the night of Ara's rod.* A flash of pain thrust into him, piercing, exquisite. Did he truly believe what he had told Timothy? Did man live beyond the days on earth, or was such a thing born of one's desire to again see those he loved? If only there were a way to know. He inwardly scoffed. No man had ever died and come back and in no other way could those who yet lived know what lay beyond — if anything.

Benjamin clamped down hard on his morbid thoughts. Why trouble himself over what he or no other could change, as did the scribes and Pharisees who spent their lives arguing over the jots and tittles of the law. Did their musings change anything? Nay. The sun still rose glorious in the east, painted the western sky with purple, rose, and gold.

"Grandfather." Two earnest black eyes stared upward. "You saw the Messiah in a dream, but I never have. How will I know when I find Him?" An anxious look crept into the childish face.

"You will know." Benjamin's heart thumped at the innocent child's use of the word *when*. "I cannot say how, Timothy, yet you will know just as you know my countenance or your father's."

"The people in Bethlehem didn't know." The small hand gripped tighter.

"Ah, but they were not looking for Him, as are we," he softly reminded.

Timothy's worried expression changed. He turned his head. "Why are all the people shouting?"

"I do not know, but we shall find out." Benjamin scooped the boy to his shoulder and raced toward the crowd gathered in front of the temple. Men swore when he pushed them aside, but an urgency caused him to continue. Timothy clung tightly, arms entwined around his grandfather's neck.

"Someone is overturning the money changers' tables!" a voice cried. "Stop him!" A hundred throats caught up the cry.

"Timothy, can you see what is happening?" Benjamin panted from the exertion of forcing himself through the crowd and into the outer courtyard. "All I see is other people."

"A man is turning tables over. He is pouring out the money. I see his back!" Timothy shrilled. He craned his neck. "He has caught up some small cords and is making a whip. Grandfather, he is driving the oxen and the sheep out of the temple." His voice rose higher. "He is driving the money changers out, too!"

The crowd quieted, as if too stunned by the scene before them to speak. In the eerie silence a voice rang, not with rage, but with commanding strength. "Is it not written, My house shall be called of all nations the house of prayer? But ye have made it a den of thieves."

Benjamin froze at the sense of familiarity that inched over him when he heard the voice. He desperately struggled forward and caught a glimpse of set shoulders. If only he could see the speaker's face! The next instant a roar like the bellow of hungry lions split the air, followed by the shouts of Romans outside the temple, demanding an explanation. Would they enter the temple of the Most High? Blasphemy!

Nay, the man who had created such havoc disappeared. One moment he stood with head raised, scourging those who transgressed. The next moment, he had gone. Benjamin remembered what Ara had said of the time in Nazareth. Jesus passed through their midst and went His way, although no one knows how.

"Wait!" Benjamin shouted. He forged through the multitudes, Timothy still perched on his shoulder. Heart heavy, he turned away.

Hours later he trudged wearily back to the camp, Timothy asleep in his strong arms. He had searched for hours, to no avail. As the cooking fires dwindled on the hillsides following the evening meal, he told his family, "Perhaps this is what my dream or vision meant. That I will only catch glimpses of Him and never see Him face to face before I die." He heaved a great sigh and sadly added, "Even when I tell myself He might not be the One I seek, yet I fear I have missed the Messiah." His voice lowered to a whisper. "Again."

"Timothy, what was he like, the man you saw?" Michal inquired.

"Tall and strong. I couldn't see his face, even though I tried." Timothy wore the same anxious look that had troubled his eyes on the way to the temple. "Grandfather, would the Messiah whip people with cords?"

"I know not. Yet what the man said is true. The money changers have made the temple a den of thieves. They pretend to find blemishes in spotless lambs and charge highly to procure one they have pronounced pure. Everyone knows that each Passover they charge the people more for lambs and doves. Soon the poor will not be able to sacrifice because of the money changers' greed. How they will hate one who dares shout their hypocrisy and dishonesty for all to hear. It is well the courageous man vanished."

Concern filled Michal's face. "Surely they

would not lay hands on Him or cause harm to befall Him!"

"They were very angry," Timothy said solemnly.

The little family didn't realize how angry until the next day. Like a swarm of hornets, people gathered in groups and discussed the man Jesus. "It is said the Teacher told those who came seeking a sign that if the temple were destroyed, in three days He would raise it up," one shouted. "Blasphemy. Death to the blasphemers." Others took up the cry. Benjamin shuddered. The reckless mood of the multitude led him to make a hasty decision.

"We will go home," he said. "If Ara were here, we would have found him by now. Neither is there any more word about Jesus. Many believe He and His disciples have left the city. In any event, Jerusalem is no place for us. Come. Let us rise and return to Bethlehem." He saw by Michal's expression how much she agreed with him. The ferment of unrest swirled like sand in a desert storm.

Passover left them with much to ponder. All the way home they talked of the events that had taken place and tried to discern their meaning. On the one hand, the man who chastised the money changers, overturned their tables, and drove out the livestock certainly had courage. "He spoke with authority," Benjamin told the others who had not been at the temple the day before. On the other hand —

"He didn't sound angry," Timothy interrupted his elders' discussion. The importance of having been the only one in the party who actually witnessed the amazing event added a cocky spring to his step. His face wrinkled into a frown. "The man in the temple sounded like my father when he has to punish me when I do something wrong." The cockiness fled in his struggle to make clear what shone in his eyes. "Father says he does it because he must, but it hurts him inside. I wonder if the man felt that way, too?"

No one replied.

Timothy hesitated, then hopped on one foot and changed the subject. "I never saw a thieves' den." He stopped long enough to allow a gap-toothed grin to spread over his face. "I saw a fox's den one time." His black eyes danced with mischief and he laughed.

So did the others and the discussion faded and died. Yet Benjamin knew hours of pondering lay ahead. A measure of peace came

141

to him. Why should he grieve? Had he not already been given more than most men? If Jehovah willed, he would one day find the Christ-child, now grown to manhood — if not in this life, surely in the next, for he would never stop believing it existed. Nay, he would put aside anxiety and wait.

In the days and weeks that followed, Benjamin found it easier than he had expected. However, a new worry clawed at his heart and mind. No further word had come from Ara. Had evil befallen him? Surely in all the time since the first message he would have found a way to send another when he knew how eager they were to hear. Suppose he had grown ill. Even now he might lie hurt or dying. Bands of wild men and robbers still infested the land and Zerah was a fine horse. Many men's eyes had covetously gleamed when they beheld the black. Try as he would to reassure himself by saying those with whom his son traveled would surely send word if anything bad happened, Benjamin could not throw aside the cloak of concern he sometimes felt would smother him.

One morning Michal lifted herself to rest on one elbow. "My husband, you must go find Ara. I have been troubled much in a dream." Her still-lovely face twisted and tearstained sheets showed she had wept in her sleep. "I know not what it is. I only know you must go. Today."

"I, too, have felt he needs me." Benjamin shut his lips and said no more. He made ready for his journey, embraced Michal, and rode up the hill Ara had climbed so long ago. A final wave to his watching wife and he started down the other side, only to pause near the spot Ara had once stopped. "Lord God of Israel, grant that I may find my son."

Many years ago Benjamin had set out on a quest, only to fail. He shivered. How many times as a shepherd boy had he left the flock and sought out the one lost sheep, the single crying lamb that had strayed? He remembered a time Ara, then a small, sturdy child, had wandered away from home. Never would the seeking father forget the glad cry, "My father, you have come!" when he discovered his son huddled behind a big rock, too proud to cry although darkness descended like rain. Ara fell asleep in the strong arms that carried and protected him. Strange, the long ago concern and his present sense of something wrong blended until Ara, the man, became again a young boy who needed his father.

"It will take the wisdom of Solomon to

find him," Benjamin muttered. "I wish I had Ebenezer." He patted his mount. "You're a fine horse, but never have I had a companion such as that ragged donkey."

Stay. Did he not perceive a companionship once felt in the fields at night? Although the sun shimmered on the road ahead, and no glorious light or figure appeared, Benjamin felt an unexplainable Presence beside him, encouraging, calling him forward.

Snatches from the psalms written by David rose naturally to his lips.

"I will lift up mine eyes unto the hills, for whence cometh my help . . . Yea, though I walk through the valley of the shadow of death I fear no evil: for Thou art with me; Thy rod and Thy staff, they comfort me. . . . Thy word is a lamp unto my feet, and a light unto my path. . . . The Lord is on my side; I will not fear. . . ."

Benjamin's spirits lifted. So long as the Presence stayed beside him, he could endure. Somewhere in the distance, perhaps in a remote, obscure spot, surely Ara awaited the father he knew would come seeking his missing son.

Part 2

nine

Sabra clutched her cloak and huddled in the midnight shadows. Fear stroked mind and soul. The clop-clop of horses' hooves outside the narrow, dark street where she hid plunged her into despair. She curled into the smallest ball possible, glad for the black night and heavy, dark garment that covered her. Unless she moved, there was little chance she would be discovered. She bit back a cry. To be found meant going back. I shall not, her heart screamed. Death is preferable to Jethro, if he finds the wench who dares refuse his bed.

A bitter smile marred her pale face. Jethro, as pre-eminent as his name. Who would believe her if she accused the man who served as advocate for his kind? Did not all Capernaum praise Jethro's cleverness in defending the rich in their "rightful claims" against the poor? Sabra sneered. Only too well did she know what those rightful claims meant. Such an accusation had ruined her father, who had been mother as well when his wife died a few years after birthing Sabra. Jethro had stripped him of dignity, jewels, and their spacious home overlooking the lovely Sea of Galilee.

Hot tears burned behind her eyelids. Sabra proudly refused to let even one fall. Had she not held them back when the final ignominy was heaped on her father, seeing his only child put into servitude, a single step above a slave? Strong men had held him back when he attempted to defend Sabra, who had beat against Jethro's minions. One had dealt her a blow that spun her to the ground.

"By Jupiter and Mars!" another exclaimed when Sabra lay moaning on the ground. "You have broken the wench's arm. Jethro will have your head."

She had seen the agony in her father's face, the way he tried to break free, even through the red haze of pain that lasted for days. The bone had been so badly shattered even the finest physicians could not repair it. Long after healing came, Sabra's arm remained crooked and withered.

Through all the turmoil, Father had also been too proud to cry. Sabra last saw him there outside the gates of the home he no longer owned. His final words before Jethro's men came were, "You are of noble birth. Never forget that and never forget your name means thorny cactus. Guard well your pride and be strong, as the desert plant is strong. It survives, nay, thrives in the harshest places." He rested one hand on her shining black hair. "The cactus blooms in spite of its surroundings. Do likewise, my beloved child."

Had Father suspected even then what lay in store for his daughter a few short years later when she reached womanhood? Perhaps, for a few days later he opened his veins, seeking death when he could not live with shame. Could she do less? Sabra slid one hand to her bosom in a barely perceptible movement. Her fingers closed on the tiny dagger hidden inside her garments, smuggled from her home when she had been taken. At the time, it meant something to cherish simply because it belonged to her father. Now it offered escape.

Would she have the courage to use the slim, keen blade? She felt color drain from her head. She must, if not to do so meant dishonor to body and soul.

The sound of the night riders faded, but she dared not move. Her cramped muscles relaxed. Exhaustion took its toll. Protected by the enveloping cloak, she slept until an inner awareness caused her to awaken with the crowing of the first cock. She must not be found here, or anywhere nearby. How could she go from the soon-to-be crowded streets without being seen?

Her dark eyes flashed. If only one of the gods in Jethro's house, those ugly idols she polished and hated, cared about servant girls. *Pah.* Even if such a god existed, which she doubted, his or her image would shatter rather than be exalted in the house of a man who forced unwelcome attentions on those who served him.

Some time earlier, the first time Jethro approached her, Sabra compelled herself to act innocent, as if she had not understood the meaning of his words. It served her well for a time, especially since a new girl had come to the household. She had proved willing, and Sabra had sighed with relief.

It had not lasted long. In the last few months, when Sabra's reflection in gleaming tile and water showed the increasing loveliness the years had bestowed on her. Jethro used every pretense to summon her. She hated the way he had laid his hand on her sleeve to detain her. It had taken all her strength to look straight into his evil eyes and every bit of her cunning to avoid contact with him. A dozen times she had considered going to his wife and had rejected the idea immediately. Too well she knew how little she would be believed. A year before, a young girl had done so. The mistress had her whipped for daring to charge the master of the house with such an unspeakable thing. Sabra knew without conceit she was favorite of all the slaves, but even that would not save her.

Did the mistress really believe Jethro as upright as he pretended? Or did she blindly refuse to admit otherwise? It didn't really matter. What counted was that this very night Jethro had for the first time come to the small room where Sabra lay sleeping. She awakened to find a dark figure kneeling by her pallet. Jethro's heavy hand covered her mouth, his voice hissed in her ear.

"Don't cry out or it will be the worse for you. Will you submit willingly?" He lifted his hand so she could reply.

For a moment Sabra lay passive, wondering if she were really awake. She could not reach the dagger that now lay near her heart even while she slept. Neither could she hope to overpower him and flee. Jethro's weight was half again her own and he possessed great fleetness of foot.

Spirit of my father, deliver me, she prayed, while a dozen wild ideas swept in and out of her mind. None could save her. Stay. Had she not the one escape even Jethro would not lightly put aside? Her face burned in the darkness, but she forced herself to say, "It cannot be. Not now." Desperate in her hour of need she faltered, "I am with the way of women." Shame scorched her. No decent woman ever mentioned such things. Yet it was her only defense. *Did he understand? He must. Would he go?* Sabra felt her life and sanity hung on his next move. If he refused to spare her, she would rouse the household, the entire neighborhood with her screams, and fight until dead or unconscious.

Jethro's body twitched. He cursed. "Is this true?"

"Master, have I ever lied to you?" She held her breath.

His hoarse whisper had barely reached her ears. "Nay." The next moment he rose to full height. "Say nothing of this. Soon things will change." He walked to the door on silent feet, leaving Sabra alone.

Waves of horror rocked her slim body. Hours later she slipped from her bed, dressed, wrapped herself in the warm, dark cloak, and snatched what few things she

152

could easily carry. Step by wary step she slipped from her room, making sure no door clicked behind her, no board beneath her feet betrayed her with a creak. She dared not seek food. A few coins carefully hoarded over the dreary months in service must stand between her and want.

Her red lips curled. Honor came before food. If she could just get away, what mattered it whether she had food or drink?

Memories of all that happened returned to the shivering girl whose eighteen years held the heights of happiness, the depths of despair. "Thorny cactus," she whispered to the pre-dawn murk. "Father said to survive and bloom. I shall try. When I cannot —" Her fingers again crept suggestively to her breast.

Cunning she had not known existed within her rose to Sabra's aid. After her first wild desire to get as far away as possible on her limited funds, she shook her head. "Nay. Jethro has spies everywhere. He will seek every caravan to see if I am with them, knowing of a certainty why I fled and how great my desire is to leave Capernaum, beautiful as it is." An exultant smile brightened her somber face. "My best protection is in doing what he expects not."

Her smile died and she rubbed her withered arm. "If only I were not marked! I must be careful never to let this be seen. All of Capernaum knew when Jethro took me to his home." She crimsoned at the knowledge. "All knew why, as well, I wager — except me." She angrily pushed aside self-pity. If she were to live with her wits, there must be no looking back. Yesterday had gone. Only the gods knew what tomorrow held. She must dwell in the tents of today.

"Suppose I cease being the pursued and turn pursuer?" she mused. "By spying on Jethro and his household. I will learn much." Fear assailed her. Even to discover what she desperately needed to know, could she force her dragging footsteps back to Jethro's home?

I must and I shall," she defiantly told the lowering sky. It heralded a storm already ruffling the waters of the Sea of Galilee. Drab and gray, each wore a hat of curling white foam. Spray flung high. There would be no fishing this day. Already waves pounded the shore, warning danger lurked in their depths for any foolish man who challenged them.

Sabra's keen mind seized on the fact. She needed a place to hide until darkness overtook the land. Spying on Jethro in daylight hours would bring instant death to her dreams of escaping his clutches. No one would look for her in a beached boat in the middle of a gale. Dozens of boats meant all the more chance of safety. Even if a rough fisherman found her crouched beneath a sail to keep off the pounding rain, he could be no worse than Jethro.

She considered allowing it to happen and shook her head. The owner might fear Jethro's power and vengeful nature, as others did, and turn her over to him. Stories ran rampant of how Jethro treated those who offended him. She must not chance risking others to save herself.

Sabra again touched her crooked arm. If it were not for that, she could easily disguise herself. She sighed. What could not be changed must be endured. Rain began, large spattering drops that settled into a deluge. Thought of comfort beneath a rough sail loomed more and more appealing. Thoroughly miserable where she was, Sabra decided to chance it. But first, she would do all she could to change her appearance. She began by withdrawing her dagger and whacking off the long, black hair she secretly loved. With ruthless fingers, she didn't stop until shorn. She longed for a mirror but had none.

Next, she scooped a handful of earth, softened by the rain. She rubbed it into her face until her cheeks stung, then wiped off the excess. A giggle slipped out. There! Once she found other clothing, she should be safe.

Never had Sabra stolen anything. Her father had taught her a thief was little better than a dog. Now necessity overcame distaste. She slipped from place to place until she found a shop where the owner stood in the doorway, gesticulating and arguing with someone in the street. With a deep breath, Sabra entered through the rear and kept low so she would not be seen above the counters. The first robes she came to were coarse, strong, suitable for men who labored with their hands. Her heart leaped. In a thrice, she discarded her garments and buried them among stacks of goods where they might not be discovered for some time.

Sabra turned to go. Nay. She could not steal, even though the shopkeeper would probably never know a paltry few of his goods had been taken. She stooped and laid a coin on the floor. If the owner thought he had dropped it, so be it. Clad in the roughest garments she had ever worn, the girl in man's clothing went out the way she came in and fled as if pursued by legions of soldiers.

No one paid the slightest attention to her. After much maneuvering, Sabra reached the shore, undetected. She crawled into a boat among many, neither the first nor the last, with a sail for a blanket. She reasoned, *Even if someone comes, it is unlikely he will examine the very boat where I hide.*

Fortune smiled on the weary girl. She fell asleep to the steady drum of rain on her frail shelter and the sound of churning waves that at last stilled. Shimmering stars peered down from their lofty perch when Sabra cautiously peeped from beneath the sail. Her stomach felt like a giant cavern and she remembered she had not eaten since the evening before. Using the utmost caution, she left the little boat. It seemed more like a home than anywhere she had been since her father died.

Where could she find food? Should she spy on Jethro before she sought sustenance? Nay. Her long fast had left her weak and unwilling to near his home. Her steps turned toward the marketplace, then stopped. If she attempted to purchase food at this hour, it would attract attention. Yet she must eat. She closed her eyes, trying to think. Unbidden came the memory of steaming bowls and cups even for the servants at Jethro's. A pink tongue licked her lips. Dared she trust one of those who served there? Some had been kind to her.

Her lips quivered and she shook her head.

She could trust no one but herself and the spirit of her dead father. Heartsick, she trudged from dark street to dark street until faintness from hunger threatened. She lingered outside a closed stall and breathed in the odor of fruit. A tiny light showed from beneath the door of the house behind it. Sabra's eyes widened. On the ground before her lay a once-golden sphere, mud-spattered from where it had fallen and lain undetected.

She grabbed the orange and retreated into the shadows. She wiped its skin and peeled it. Never had anything tasted better. New hope surged through her. Nearly twenty-four hours had gone by. So far, she remained free.

"Now to learn what Jethro is doing," she murmured. By dint of streets she had begun to know as never before, she reached the brightly lit house. Hours later she rose and stumbled away, sick at heart. Would it not have been better never to know the web Jethro had already begun to weave in order to find her? From her listening post just outside an open window, Sabra had heard her enemy promise great rewards to a band of ruffians whose greedy faces burst into smiles.

"Never!" she told the night sky. "Am I an

ostrich who sticks her head in the earth and thinks she is hidden? I am a woman and I will best Jethro."

She slept that night in another secluded spot and the next day ventured into the marketplace and purchased a few easily carried stores: dates, cheese, a little bread, and a small piece of dried fish. She had no way to cook and portioned out her food carefully. Starvation faced her when she used the last of her coins and her father's daughter should never beg bread.

Weeks passed. Sabra hadn't realized to what lengths hunger drove one. On a night when the heavens opened, the girl's pride lay in the mud. In order to survive, she must eat. So be it. She would walk until she could go no farther then knock on a door and plead for food like the beggar she had become.

A shred of caution remained. Choosing the wrong place meant the miserable weeks of avoiding Jethro were all in vain. She passed by palaces and mansions. She hesitated before cottages, went on to huts and hovels. Gradually she worked her way to the uttermost edge of Capernaum. Here, space separated the few dwelling places. Sabra realized without being told only the lowliest, most humble persons lived in the rude buildings. When she saw no more dim lights ahead to signify other huts, she took a deep breath and timidly knocked on the door of the least pretentious of all. Sabra felt she could never again muster up courage to ask for help if the householder refused to give her shelter and food.

The door opened a crack. A little old woman peered out. "What is it?" She held a lamp with a bit of oil. Its rays shone on the stranger.

"Good mother, I am hungry and cold," Sabra choked out. "Have you a bite of bread and a corner where I might rest?" She leaned weakly against the door frame and blinked in the lamplight, unable to see if suspicion rested on the old woman's face.

"Child, you wear man's garments, yet speak with the voice of a woman."

"I fear a man, so I disguise myself," Sabra mumbled.

"Daughter, come in." The door opened wide. A thin arm gently tugged on Sabra's arm and led her into a single room whose warmth made the girl feel she had stumbled into the heaven some believed existed.

The spirit that had kept her going her lone road for weeks failed her. Despite the evidences of poverty, Sabra felt safe. Her knees buckled. She vaguely heard soft mur-

murs, felt a damp cloth wipe her face clean for the first time since she left Jethro's. Warm broth slid down Sabra's parched throat. Her hostess guided her to a narrow cot. The spent girl fell onto it and blackness swallowed her.

Late the next day, she awakened, face wrinkled in puzzlement. Where was she? She opened her eyes. Memory returned. Fear replaced the feeling of peace that had prevailed the night before. She gazed down at herself in horror. Gone were the clothes that protected her identity. She lay clad only in a rough, homespun gown. A sound of dismay burst from her lips. The old woman who undressed her had seen the withered arm!

"There's nothing here to frighten you, child." In the late afternoon sunshine that shone through the open door, the little old woman looked like an aged angel. The rays turned her white hair to gold. "I am Joanna, meaning God is gracious, which He is. Few come to trouble me. Those who come, do not enter my hut. You are safe from all harm." Her tranquil eyes radiated peace.

"You know who I am?" Sabra held her breath and picked at the coverlet with nervous fingers.

"A child who came to me in the storm." Joanna smiled, a real mother's smile that

161

sank deep into her visitor's heart. "A child who has found a home so long as she needs or wants it."

The acceptance in her words and face undermined the wall Sabra had erected around herself in order to survive. "I must tell you about me. When you know — everything — you will drive me away.

"Nay, I shall give thanks to Jehovah for sending you to cheer my lonely days." Joanna shook her head decidedly and ladled broth into a cracked bowl. "Eat first. Then you may tell me as much or as little as you like."

Sabra found it far easier than she had expected. Although she bowed her head when she came to the part about Jethro, she bravely related the incidents of the terrible night and its aftermath. "I must rise and go," she said sadly. "If he finds I am here, he will do something dreadful to you. It is his way."

"If you were my daughter, think you I would be afraid of what men could do to me? Child, what are you called?"

"Sabra. It means thorny cactus."

Joanna's eyes brightened. "There is another meaning, as well: to rest. Abide with me, daughter, at least until you decide what to do."

"If only I could!" She swept a glance around the little room and reddened. "You — I — you gave me your cot."

"A pallet on the floor serves as well." The dignity in the old woman's eyes stilled Sabra's protests. "As you will learn this night when we exchange places."

"I have no money or food." The girl's head drooped in shame.

"We shall be fed from my garden and I have a little goat who gives milk. When you are rested you shall learn to care for her, if you like."

So their friendship began, and the love that within days made the words mother and daughter far more than a commonly used expression.

ten

"Joanna." Sabra yanked a stubborn weed from the patch of garden behind the hut where she had found refuge. "Why do you not have gods in your dwelling place? Jethro had many."

"Did they make him a better man?"

"Nay." Sabra's sun-warmed face shadowed. She clasped her grubby hands.

"What good are gods who have no power to change men's lives and hearts? I serve the one true God, Jehovah. He is the only One worthy of our worship. He it is who made land, sea, sky, and all within them."

"You have no graven image of Him." Sabra rocked back on her heels.

"Such things are forbidden. Jehovah is a jealous God."

"How can you worship a god you have not seen?" the girl marveled. She passed an earth-stained hand over her face and left a black streak on one cheek.

"My child, even the blind can see with the heart — all that is around them."A faraway expression crept into the old eyes. "Never do I behold a new day without feeling Him near. Every sunrise, each storm over the Sea of Galilee, the raging winds and quiet sunsets proclaim the work of His hands."

A wistful longing stole into Sabra's soul. "Your invisible God is hard to imagine. If only He . . ." She could not speak the words that hovered just behind her white teeth.

Joanna smiled. Her face burst into a hundred wrinkles. "Ah, you long to see Him face to face. We shall. Soon. Have you not heard of the coming of the Messiah, the One who will deliver His people?"

Sabra's head drooped like a wilted flower. "I know nothing of a Messiah. If there indeed be one, what has He to do with me — hunted and afraid?"

"Do you not believe more than chance caused you to knock at my door?"

She wrinkled her forehead. "Perhaps the gods smiled on me, for once."

The older woman laughed. "The ugly idols of Jethro's you confessed you hated?" Her deep-set eyes twinkled. "If those lifeless images of clay and metal could control actions, which they cannot, who would they be more inclined to aid? A runaway servant? Or the master of the house who bows and places offerings before them?"

Sabra's dark eyes opened wide. A thrill went through her. "You really believe your God led me to you?"

"Yea. Did I not need someone to help me with the garden and milk the little goat, now that many years are upon me?" A sweet smile spread over the aged countenance. "Child, you fill the place of a daughter."

"And you are the only mother I have ever known." Sabra's lips quivered. She impulsively rose, laid one arm around the old woman's thin shoulders, and laid her head against the white hair. In doing so, the sleeve of the rough garment she wore while working in the garden fell back, revealing her withered arm.

"Joanna, if only it were not for this arm, I think I could escape Jethro forever. He will surely seek me among those who travel from Capernaum."

"I pray it will be so."

Something in Joanna's voice loosened Sabra's hold. She stepped back and looked full into the face made wise by years and faith in the God unknown to her companion. "You fear his minions may come here?"

Joanna sighed. Compassion softened her gaze. "Jethro is not one to easily give up that which he believes is his. When he learns you did not go with a caravan, his passions will rise. Jehovah alone knows what he will do, how far-reaching his search for you will be." She patted Sabra's hand. "My prayers for your protection are many and will surely be heard. You have been safe here many weeks. Grant it may continue to be."

Some of Sabra's fear subsided. Her cropped hair and rude clothing changed her appearance mightily. Only the crooked arm betrayed her and did she not keep it well covered on the rare occasions when someone came to the hut? Joanna had steadfastly refused to allow her to go even to the closest well.

At last she rebelled. "Jethro himself could not recognize me. Today I go with you." Nothing Joanna could say dissuaded her. They carefully chose a time, so early few would be abroad. Shapeless in Joanna's rough cloaks, heads bent, they approached the well. A single person sat close by, face turned toward the east as if waiting for the morning sun.

"Peace," Joanna mumbled, keeping her gaze cast down.

Sabra could scarcely believe the joy that came to the man's face. He bounded to his feet and leaped into the air. "Peace, say you? What know you of peace?" Tears poured to the dusty street beneath his sandaled feet. "There is only one peace and it is Jesus, the carpenter of Nazareth." He rushed on without waiting for an answer.

"Was I not cursed with a spirit of an unclean devil that tormented me day and night? Did it not cry out with a loud voice, 'Let us alone; what have we to do with Thee, Thou Jesus of Nazareth? Art Thou come to destroy us? I know who Thou art; the Holy One of God.'"

The man's face reflected the first ray of sun in the tranquil sky. "When Jesus spoke with such power and authority, commanding the devil to depart my body, I knew the hour of death had come. At the very moment when I thought I would perish, freedom came." He leaped again. "Praise His holy name forever! I cannot follow Him, but I shall sit by the well and tell all who will listen."

"The unclean spirit has not returned?"

"Nay." He flung his arms to the pinkening sky, eyes clear and understanding. "You cannot know peace unless you have lived without it. But that is not all."

Sabra found herself transfixed as much by the look in his face as the story.

The man lowered his voice and looked both ways to make sure no one overheard. "Jesus left the synagogue and went to a follower's house. The mother of Simon Peter's wife lay burning with fever." His voice dropped to a whisper and a glory not of the world came to his face. "He stood over her, rebuked the fever and it left her. She immediately arose and ministered unto them. It is said Jesus heals diverse diseases. As many as come to Him, He lays His hands on every one and heals them."

A wild thought entered Sabra's heart. She opened her lips to cry out. Joanna's quick nudge stopped her. She saw warning in her friend's face.

"Peace unto you, my son."

"And to you." The man clasped his hands and bowed his head.

Sabra silently drew the water. She filled two buckets for herself, half-filled one for Joanna. As soon as they were out of the man's hearing she whispered. "Mother, why did you stop me? I longed to ask if this Jesus had ever healed a withered arm."

"I sensed it. You must not. If we find Jesus and He heals your infirmity, it is best not even the man at the well knows. He is so filled with the spirit of the Lord he cannot still his tongue. One day he might mention it in praise and be heard by one of Jethro's spies. Daughter, listen to the words of an old woman. We will seek out this man Jesus in the midst of the multitude."

"Are you able?"

Joanna straightened. Sabra blinked. Had years dropped from her rescuer's shoulders? She held her breath.

"Strength will be given. Surely this man must be the Messiah. Who else could cast out devils, heal the sick? Come, we must go home now. Later I shall return to the well, at the time of day as is my custom. You must not go then." She chuckled and the sound reminded Sabra of wind in the dry grass. "My ears hear well. I will learn more of this Jesus."

Joanna came home at a pace Sabra wouldn't have believed possible. Her half-filled bucket slopped water with every step. "Hurry, we must find Jesus before He leaves. Idle gossip has it He will depart soon."

If she lived to be older than Rome itself, Sabra could never forget what followed. She and Joanna started out but before they had gone a mile into their journey the aged woman stopped. "I cannot go fast enough," she brokenly said. "You must go without me. Nay, do not dispute. Make your way to Jesus and kneel at His feet, asking for healing. Go, Sabra. Then return that I may know if Jesus of Nazareth is truly the Messiah. First, bow your head."

Wondering, Sabra obeyed. She felt gnarled hands on her veiled hair. She heard Joanna's quickened breathing slow, then words of blessing flowed over her. The petition for safety and success in her quest warmed the girl.

"Rise and go, Sabra. Peace."

She could not question the authority in Joanna's voice. Blinded by emotion, she set her face away from the only safety she had known in years to find a Jewish Messiah she was not sure she believed existed. Yet as her friend had said, who else had the power on earth or in heaven to heal, to free? The best evidence to Jesus being the awaited One lay in the feelings stirred by the man at the well. A quickening she had never experienced rose and threatened to smother her. Sabra sped up, impelled by the sense of urgency in Joanna's parting.

At last she came to where He taught. Her spirits sank. She could not get through the throngs who swarmed around Him. Calling out did little good for others also called. Never had she seen such suffering. Blind beggars, guided by children in ragged clothing. Men and women on litters, held aloft by sweating men who carried them. Those with twisted limbs, who staggered forward with the help of crude sticks. Some whose eyes showed they had no reason. All had one thing in common: they struggled to reach Jesus.

"Unclean! Unclean!" A high-pitched cry came through the crowd.

"Make way for the leper!" A man near Sabra sprang back. Others did the same, creating a path through the frightened crowd. No one dared touch a leper for fear of also being afflicted.

Hope weakened, died. Sabra's heart sickened within her. The moment the leper got through, the ranks would close behind him. She could not reach Jesus.

She never knew why she glanced up at that moment. Disappointment changed to terror. A few rods away stood a man she knew only too well: one of the ruffians Jethro had promised riches if he should find her. How or why he came to be there, she knew not, but something inside her snapped. She ducked her head. He had not yet seen her. She must escape — but how? Even now the leper came closer. In a moment he would pass.

Desperation drove Sabra. She timed her movements well. The instant the man came even with her, she thrust her way toward him and darted into the space behind the man who still cried, "Unclean." It drew unwelcome attention to her. Curses and protests came from the angered crowd. She didn't falter, but trod almost on the leper's garment. No one attempted to seize her. It meant the risk of bringing the curse to any-one so foolish.

Sabra's heart furiously pounded when she stood before Jesus. Dimly aware of the crowd who screamed the news a leper had been made well, she saw only His gaze. Nay, in it reflected all she was and had ever been. She forgot her withered arm, the need for caution, and fell to her knees before Him. Hot tears fell on his dusty, sandaled feet. "Forgive me for not believing in You," she whispered from an overflowing heart.

A gentle hand touched Sabra's head. She didn't know if Jesus spoke. If so, how could she hear above the screaming multitude? Yet the words "Peace, daughter" rang in her mind. The hand lifted. Sabra felt the same desertion she knew when word came of her father's blood-letting. She stumbled away on unsteady legs, fighting against the tide of humanity that surged toward Jesus as a hart scrambles from the depths to mountain heights. Minutes, hours, or a lifetime later, she found herself alone, clothing and veil awry. Forgetful of the need for caution, Sabra dropped to the ground and buried her face in her hands.

"I have seen Him. Nothing will ever be the same," she said in hushed tones. Only a bird on the wing answered her, its plaintive cry piercing the trance-like state she had been in since first gazing into the Messiah's eyes. Sabra started, looked around. Lazy shadows grayed the hillsides and warned evening was nigh. She slowly stood and raised her hands to straighten her veil. The wide sleeves of her cloak fell away from her wrists.

Blood drained from Sabra's head. She tottered, unable to comprehend. She closed her eyes tightly and forced them open once more. One hand crept to her bosom where the dagger yet lay. She freed it and ruthlessly touched its razor-sharp blade to one finger. A drop of bright blood stood out on her skin.

Nay, she dreamed not. Sabra raised her arms again and stared at them. Soiled with travel, they blurred behind a shimmer of tears. Round. Firm. Straight.

Sabra fell to her knees. "When, oh, Lord? I failed to ask."

Peace unlike anything she had experienced poured into her soul. Joanna's words from many weeks returned: *Sabra. At rest.* Like a weary child who has returned to its father after a long, long time, she slept.

A legion of birds awakened her at early light. Her heart joined in praise to their Creator. Little heeding hunger pangs or rumpled clothing, she sprang to meet the new day. "I didn't even thank Him," she told the birds. Regret filled her. "I must find and follow Him. Surely, He is the Messiah, as Joanna —"

Joanna! All her happy plans vanished like black cats in the night. "How can I leave Joanna, who waits for me even now?" she cried. "Yet how can I not follow Jesus?" Torn between desire and duty, she knelt and offered the first real prayer in her life. "Please, help me."

She remembered the expression in Jesus' eyes. If He were here now, what would He tell her she must do? Gradually, her turmoil ceased. Hours later, she turned from the tempting road that led to Jesus and started back the way she had come. Strange. The pitfalls that had loomed so large on her earlier journey seemed as naught. Neither did she feel the terrible loss expected. In its place, a gentle memory of One who laid His hand on her head walked beside her.

When she neared her destination, Sabra felt a return of caution. She waited until dusk hid her to pass the well. A half mile from Joanna's, she heard a rustling in the bushes. Senses alive from all she had experienced, she strained to listen. The rustling came again, a furtive sound that thrust red-hot fear into her.

"Is it you?" A low voice asked from the gloom.

"Joanna! What — ?"

"Shh." A surprisingly strong hand pulled her aside and behind a clump of bushes. "A man came asking for you."

Sabra gasped, feeling she had tumbled from a high tower into a black pit.

"He learned a girl accompanied me to the well," Joanna went on. "He asked if she had long, dark hair and much beauty."

"What did you say?" Sabra's fingers dug into the other's arms like talons.

Joanna didn't flinch. "I said the girl who had been with me for a time had ragged hair and a dirty face. I told him she had gone, I knew not where."

"You spoke falsely to save me?"

Joanna chuckled. "Nay. I had no way of knowing where you were at the very moment I spoke. He went away. Yet I am not sure he has really gone. I have heard the nicker of a horse since he departed."

Sabra's hold relaxed. "This is why you met me here?"

"Yea. Come." She led the girl to the hut, twisting among trees and bushes rather than going straight to the door. Once there she paused. "It is well." Yet inside she whispered, "We shall make no light this night." Longing lay in her voice. "Daughter, did you find Jesus? Is He the Messiah?"

Sabra wanted to shout with joy and dared not. She knelt on the earthen floor beside the bed Joanna had given her the night she came. "Yea." A rush of feeling prevented further speech. She wordlessly grasped Joanna's hands and placed one on each of her own strong, young arms. "I am made whole."

Joanna stiffened. Her hands stroked Sabra's arms. "He is the Messiah?"

"I believe He must be. Mother, before I reached Jesus, He healed another. That man was a leper." She swallowed and leaned her head in Joanna's lap. "I myself saw the fresh, pink skin on the leper's face and on the hands he raised in praise. The multitude shouted. I know it is true. I saw it!"

Far into the night they talked. Joanna made Sabra repeat every detail over and over. She could not get enough of hearing. At last they slept, she on her cot, Sabra on the pallet. The whinny of a horse and a loud knock roused them.

Pleasant dreams fled. Joanna left her bed, motioning Sabra to stay out of sight. She opened the door a crack. "What want you of me? Have I not told you what you asked? Why trouble you a woman old enough to die long ago?"

A rough oath followed. "I want a look at the wench who came back last night. If she is the one Jethro seeks, death is pleasant compared with his wrath."

Sabra reached for her dagger. She would protect Joanna, no matter how high the cost. The memory of watching eyes left her hand in mid-air. Reproach replaced compassion. Her hand fell to her side. She could not kill, not when that look haunted her. Better to give herself up than have it turn to sorrow.

She took a step toward the door. Stay! Excitement coursed through her veins. Jesus had given her all she needed! A smile tilted her lips. She quickly snatched earth from the floor and rubbed it on face, hands, and arms. She tousled her hair until it stood out like frayed rope. Sabra strode to the door and rudely thrust Joanna aside before opening it. She drew her eyebrows together in a fearsome frown, half-closed her eyes, and dropped her voice to guttural tones. "Ye wants me?" She screwed her mouth into a twisted grin.

"Jupiter and Mars," the pursuer exclaimed. He took a step back and surveyed her with disfavor. Two chins sagged as he grimaced.

"Never seen a wench, have ye?" She tittered.

"Not one like you. By the gods, you be the ugliest thing I ever saw." He shook his head. "Jethro would hang me to the nearest tree if I brought you to him." He started away. Stopped. A cunning look crept into his fat face. "Just to make certain, hold out your arm. The wench I seek has a crooked limb."

She held out one arm and defiantly pushed her sleeve up. "My limbs crooked? Nay. They be straighter than yer tongue." Had she gone too far in her eagerness to convince him?

"The other arm," he barked. He grabbed it, pushed her sleeve up and stared. "Pah, you're no more Jethro's plaything than I am!" He dropped her arm, turned on his heel, and marched to his horse. Not once did he look back. The clatter of hooves drummed, faded, and died.

"Praise to Jehovah." Joanna fell to her stiffened knees. "The Lord God of Israel has delivered us this day."

"Will he come back?" Danger past, Sabra felt curiously empty.

"What will he find? A poor old woman, and a fearful looking girl with two strong but dirty arms!" Joanna's sense of humor returned. "Ah, but you played your part well, my child. Even I blinked when I saw and heard you."

A tapestry of serenity descended on the little hut. No more inquisitive men came. The next weeks alone with the old woman, Sabra decided, were what heaven must be like, if indeed there were one. Even when the goat chewed through her rope and made havoc of the garden, Sabra only laughed.

Joanna's response had not been so cheerful. "I fear we must portion our food if we are to survive until it grows again." she said. "I have nothing to sell."

Sabra guiltily thought of her dagger, the only thing she possessed that could bring in coins. She had never mentioned it to

Joanna. "I will part with it rather than allow her to go hungry," Sabra muttered to the unrepentant goat. She drove her into the shed and secured the door. No longer would Mistress Goat be allowed out unless Sabra kept watch over the garden.

A pang went through her. The dagger represented all she had left of the happy days with her father. Once she had planned to use it rather than go back to Jethro. She knew now she could not. The one look into Jesus' eyes and the memory of the disappointment she fancied that day when Jethro's hireling came had taught her that. Never would she do anything to bring that expression into His eyes. Strange. She felt even if she never saw Him again, He would always know her deeds. If He did not, Jehovah would.

Sabra shrugged. Life with Joanna left little time for fanciful thinking. Weeds sprang up in the garden as if conjured. The hut must be kept tidy. Rents in garments required careful mending to make them last; the companions had no means to buy cloth.

If at times Sabra longed for something more than her quiet life, she kept it in her heart. She refused to look toward a time without Joanna.

Not so the good woman. One afternoon

when storm clouds united and the clash of thunder warned of an attack on the earth, Joanna folded her hands. "Fear not," she softly said. "One day when I am no longer here, Jehovah will care for you. I have dreamed much, Sabra. I believe great happiness lies in your future.

The girl trembled. Her own dreams of late had been troubled, threatening the calm she had known since she first looked into her Lord's face.

eleven

Ara laid aside the finished letter to his parents and rose to full height. His sinuous grace, dark mane of hair, and tawny skin resembled the lion from which he took his name. How Father and Mother would rejoice when they received word of the strange events at Cana and Nazareth! White teeth flashed in his black beard. Tomorrow he and Zerah would take the trail leading to Jesus, who was the Messiah. Yea, He must be. No man could turn water to wine or vanish from the midst of an angry crowd unless he were a god. "He is also the baby of whom the angels sang in the fields," Ara said.

He fell into a reverie. Ara possessed a deep reverence for things of the spirit. Memory of the wife and child he had lost brought pain. Yet his father's belief in another life offered hope. Now he had been chosen to fulfill his father's quest. Pleasure flowed through him like the Jordan River swelled with rain. His heart raced. The moment he found Jesus he would send for his family. Surely the Master would find Michal worthy of healing.

Ara packed and mounted Zerah before daylight. Companions had proved too slow for his driving desire. He journeyed alone except for his horse. As Benjamin once talked to gray Ebenezer, his son talked to the black. "How fortunate it is you are named for the dawn. It is the best part of the day. When all the world has risen, the roads grow dusty and noisy from the swarming crowds." He looked around in approval. Heavy dew sparkled on bushes along the road. Wraith-like mist obscured the surrounding hills. A cool quiet pervaded the air. Only the calling of birds broke the early morning hush. On such a morning had Jehovah walked with Adam in the Garden of Eden, before sin entered the world and made captives of its inhabitants? Ara's heart thrilled. Before the day ended, would he stand before the Son of the Almighty God, the Deliverer?

Zerah whickered, raised his beautiful head, and pranced a bit. Ara patted him. "You are enjoying this mission as much as I, I think." He sobered and a frown gathered above his keen, watchful eyes. Many traveled the roads, not all upright and honest. Only the day before a man with glittering eyes had sidled up to Ara, stared at his horse, and offered to buy him. He named a purchase price, so preposterous Ara laughed in the covetous face. "Sell Zerah? Never. Especially for that paltry sum." Hatred had mingled with the naked greed in the man's eyes. Ara rode on, glad they would be in Capernaum soon and off the dangerous roads. Before the sun reached its peak, Ara rode into the village.

Long ago Benjamin had learned he could get news at the village well. His son also depended on those at the well to furnish him with what he must know. Throughout the day, a steady stream of people came. Maidens and wives, with buckets and water pots. Weary travelers. Those who gleaned information from wayfarers who sought to quench their thirst. Ara watered Zerah, refreshed himself, and turned to a man who stood nearby, arms crossed and watching. "Is the man Jesus here?" Ara asked.

"Who inquires?" Suspicion oozed from every inch of his cloaked body.

Ara looked straight into the man's face. "One who seeks the Messiah."

Glory burst into the other's countenance. "He is not here, but He has been. Am I not

185

a living witness to His mercy?" The man leaped into the air.

"You know Him, then?"

"Know Him! Because of Him I live, as I did not when the unclean spirit dwelt in me." Words tumbled out in the same story he related to Joanna and Sabra. He finished by saying, "I sit by the well and tell my story. Son, do you seek healing?"

"Not for myself. For my mother, who weakens with each day. Will Jesus heal her if she comes to Him?" Ara held his breath, waiting for the answer.

"It is said He heals all who come to Him." The man dropped his voice in awe. "Even lepers."

Ara's jaw dropped. "Lepers?" Eagle wings of reason beat against hope. Had the madness the man professed had been taken from him returned? Even the smallest child knew in all the world there was no cure for leprosy.

The clearness of the other's gaze stilled the doubt. "Jesus heals them. They go about the land praising Him and showing themselves without spot or blemish, pronounced clean by the priests!" He paused. "I can take you this day to another Jesus healed. He had palsy, for which there also is no cure, as you must know."

"Sir, my gratitude will be great if you do so." Ara felt his blood quicken. Until now the miracles of Jesus had been related to Him by those who had seen. This day had he spoken with a simple man whose life would never be the same because Jesus passed by, stopping long enough to touch him. Soon he would speak with another. He followed his guide, tied Zerah in the shade of a nearby tree where any attempt to steal him would be overheard, and entered a rude hut.

Seated on a wooden stool, Ara listened — and believed. Every word brought certainty Jesus was the Messiah. The storyteller's face glowed with an unearthly light when he brokenly said, "When I heard the carpenter had returned to Capernaum, every bone in my shaking body cried out to reach Him. Had I not talked with this man who even now brings you to me?" A smile spread across his face. "Ah, you cannot know how it is to have health unless you have not known it." He held out his arms, steady as the rocks along the way Ara had come.

"My friends carried me to where He taught. We could not get near the door for the multitudes of those like me who came seeking His touch. I sensed He could make me free if I could be in His presence." His eyes glistened. Again Ara felt his heartbeat grow rapid.

"The friends I love as brothers suggested a desperate idea. They removed part of the roof above Jesus and lowered my bed until it sat on the floor before Him!" The man licked his lips and his voice grew louder.

A picture rose in Ara's mind: bold determined men whose love for their friend required taking great chances. "What happened?" he demanded.

A gleam came to the healed man's eyes. "Jesus said, 'Son, thy sins be forgiven thee.'"

Ara gasped. He leaped to his feet in protest, sending the stool clattering to the floor. "Blasphemy! Only God can forgive sin. Satan himself makes no such claim. I will hear no more." He turned blindly toward the door, more shaken than at any time in his life. How ironic for his long search, and his father's, to end at the very moment he had most believed! A lump of lead formed in the pit of his stomach and he reeled. How could he tell Benjamin? And what of Michal? There would be no healing for her. Perhaps it was all a hoax, a plan to gather credulous persons into a mighty force that would sweep Jesus into power.

"Sit down, my son." The man from the well righted the overturned stool and grasped Ara's arm. "Do this man the courtesy of listening to all of his story."

"I have no desire to hear lies." Ara scornfully looked at the second man.

"I do not lie." Like pearls from a broken string, the words dropped into the silence. "I beg of you. Hear me out."

Ara stumbled to the stool, more from the need to sit down than any wish to remain. His knees felt too weak to hold him. His hands trembled as if he were the one afflicted by the palsy.

"When Jesus made the amazing statement, I gaped at him. Why would He say such a thing when I had come to be healed? Yet a flood of warmth began inside me. What if He did not choose to heal my body? It no longer seemed important. I did not think to challenge His authority." He paused significantly.

"Like you, others did, accusing Him in their minds, for He said, 'Why reason ye these things in your hearts? Whether is it easier to say to the sick of the palsy, Thy sins be forgiven thee: or to say, Arise, and take up thy bed, and walk? But that ye may know that the Son of man hath power on earth to forgive sins, I say unto thee, Arise, and take up thy bed, and go thy way into thine house."

Ara shook his head to stop his mind from whirling. He leaned forward, gripped the speaker's hand in his powerful one, and hoarsely said, "Say on."

Some of the excitement at reliving those moments changed to calm. The man's face worked. "I lay paralyzed with fear, not sure if I could do what he commanded. The warmth within me spread, bringing strength to my limbs. I got to my feet, so." He slowly stood. "I took up my pallet, to be used only for sleeping from that time. I hastened through the multitude, rejoicing, blessing the name of the Most High for my wholeness but most of all, that my sins had fled like sheep from a marauder." Long after the man from whom devils had been cast led Ara back to the well, they could hear the other's voice raised in thanks.

Ara beheld the western sky and blinked. How could it be? Day had fled while he spoke with the two men. It did not matter. This day would remain with him forever, set apart by those moments of high hope and dark despair.

"I wanted you to hear from him what happened," his guide said simply. The setting sun bathed him in brilliance. "Each man can best tell his own story of meeting the Master. Someday, you will tell yours. Ask me not how or what, when or where. I know not. It may not be of demons or palsy. It may be the forgiving of sin or the healing of a broken heart. Whatever comes, it will be yours alone. You will share with others as we gladly shared with you today, yet every man's encounter with Jesus is different. Peace be unto you." He hesitated and glanced at the darkening sky. "Will you not share my cottage?"

"Nay. I must travel on. I can go a little way before darkness falls. I thank you for you have given more than food or shelter. You have given me hope." He untied Zerah and easily swung onto his back. "Friend, and friend you truly are, do you believe this man Jesus is truly the Son of God?"

Dignity rested on the tranquil face that reflected the sky colors painted by the Master Artist. "If He is not the Son of God, who is He? Some say He is only a good man, a bit deluded, but a great teacher. Nay. Does a good man speak as though he and his father in heaven are one? Such a thing is a lie.

"Many consider Him mad." He spread his hands wide in supplication. "Does a madman have healing powers, the power to forgive sin? Does he go about doing good and ask no gain except the hearts of those he teaches? I say unto you again, nay." A slow smile brightened his tired face. "Jesus is neither a deluded teacher nor a madman. I believe He must be the Son of God, the Messiah promised through the ages." The last words came as a whisper.

"Where shall I look for him?" Ara's broad chest felt tight.

"He is said to teach beside the Sea of Galilee. Do not be discouraged if He is not there. It is nearly Passover time; He may have gone to Jerusalem. I have not heard of Him for many weeks."

Ara snorted in disgust. "By the time I get there Passover will long be ended. I should have thought of that, gone there and waited."

"Would you wish to have missed this day?" His companion raised his hand in a blessing of peace and walked away. His words hovered in the still air.

Ara sat silently, considering all he had learned. Even though Jesus might be many miles away, a cheerful whistle rose to his lips. The prophecy of his one day finding Jesus and gaining a story of his own glowed in his heart like a sapphire in the sun. The word made him aware how fast darkness had encroached. Why had he not accepted his guide's invitation? He peered into the shadows but could not discern where he had gone. Perhaps he should approach the one healed of the palsy. Nay, for his hut was tiny and Ara had no desire to leave Zerah in the street during the long, dark hours when evil men did their thieving.

"We'll find a safe spot and share a bed," Ara whimsically told Zerah. "It won't be the first time." He started down a lane. A voice challenged him.

"Halt! Who goes there?"

Ara quailed even while wondering at the lack of animosity or arrogance in the question. Yet caution born of watching and protecting his sheep in the fields prompted him to respond, "A shepherd from Judaea."

In the fading light, a large Roman soldier stepped forward, spear in hand. He peered closely into Ara's face and appeared satisfied. "What have you to do with my master?"

"Your master? I know him not."

"Then why are you here?"

Again the lack of enmity allayed Ara's fears, born of stories about how the Roman soldiers killed the children long ago. "I seek a carpenter." He waited. If the Roman knew of Jesus he would catch the hidden meaning. If not, he would jeer and think Ara sought a kinsman.

"Come with me." The soldier parted the bushes and led Ara to a nearby bench. In whispers he said, "We are near an encampment. There are quarters nearby and we must not be overheard. Do you seek Jesus of Nazareth?"

"Yea."

"I had to make sure. There are so many spies . . . ever since Jesus healed the centurion's servant."

"A Roman centurion's servant was healed?" Ara gasped.

The soldier nodded. "Shh. I cannot explain it. I thought the Jewish prophets despised Romans. Then the servant who has long served the centurion fell ill. Although the centurion commands a full hundred soldiers, he loves that servant as a mother does her newborn babe. No man dares raise a hand against him.

"The servant was so ill with palsy we feared he would die. Some of our men reported strange happenings concerning the carpenter. One told the centurion. He mounted and rode away. I followed — against orders, I admit." His whisper turned hoarse. "He rode straight to Jesus. I felt the two were akin! My centurion represented all the authority of Rome; the carpenter's eyes showed strength seldom seen in any man. I missed their first words but crept close and nearly betrayed my presence in my amazement.

"The centurion, who tells soldiers when to come, where to go, said he was not worthy for Jesus to come under his roof. He said he believed if Jesus would but speak a word, the servant would be healed."

Ara felt sweat crawl down his neck. "What did Jesus say?"

Wonder changed to pride. "That He had not found so great a faith in all of Israel! He told the centurion to go his way; as he believed, so it would be done. I followed a distance behind on the way back, not daring think what would happen to the Nazarene when what He prophesied did not come to pass. If He had touched the servant, a spell could be cast to make him think he was healed. But not to see the man? Pah, such a thing could not be. The centurion would send us to take the false prophet once we arrived home."

Ara could not speak. His blood iced. He longed to clap his hands over his ears and shut out the death sentence he knew would come. Nay, for the soldier clutched his arm and continued.

"I cannot explain it, but when we arrived, the servant went about his duties caring for the master's household. We learned he had been healed in the same hour the carpenter predicted!"

Ara's throat constricted. "How do you explain it?"

The other didn't hesitate. "Explain it? I don't try. I have pondered it a hundred, nay, a thousand times. It makes me wonder. If Jesus heals a Roman soldier's servant, does He also care for other Romans, other soldiers? What has a Jewish Messiah — and some say that is who He is — to do with Romans?"

Black velvet night replaced the shadows. The hoarse voice continued, strangely subdued. "Since that time, word has traveled far. Scribes and priests come here. Some make jests about our centurion seeking out a Jewish impostor. Yet none can deny the unalterable fact: the servant is whole. It makes me uneasy. If Rome hears of this, the centurion's career hangs in the balance. That is why I exercised caution until the spirit within me said you could be trusted." Longing for reassurance lay in the voice of the faithful soldier who kept vigil for the superior he obviously loved.

Ara grasped the Roman's hand and leaned close. "I too have seen and heard things, even this day." He related them in whispers that carried no farther than Zerah, who had stuck his nose inside the bushes to nudge Ara's shoulder.

The big soldier listened and asked eager questions. "Then He must be who they say. Don't you see? If He is —" He never finished his sentence. Instead he leaped to attention, gripped Ara's arm, dragged him from the bushes, and shoved him toward Zerah. "Danger," he hissed. Then —

"On your way, you sniveling beggar. There is no bread or meat here for such as you." He half flung Ara onto Zerah's back. "Flee, dog, before I run you through with my spear." A coarse laugh followed.

Bewildered by the change, Ara touched his heels to Zerah. The black, made skittish by the circle of men who surrounded them, whinnied and ran — but not before Ara felt a strong handclasp and heard a barely audible whisper, "Peace."

Ara slowed Zerah to a walk after a few leaps into the protective darkness. Wise in the ways of animals, he allowed the black to choose the way. A howling wind had risen, unnoticed until now. It grated on Ara's already frayed nerves and set them on edge. He felt on the brink of a great discovery, stunned by the revelations of the day, especially those of the Roman soldier. His spirit warred between race hatred and the comradeship he had felt with the man who also struggled to understand Jesus.

A crash of distant thunder roused him after a time. "We must find shelter," he told Zerah. "Shortly, the heavens will split and empty." Shoulders hunched, he stroked his faithful horse's neck. Zerah trudged ahead on the unknown path, the dust beneath his feet turning to mud. He snorted and continued until Ara reined him in. A tiny, flickering light shone from a hut, as if a single candle stub attempted to light the ebony world in which they rode.

twelve

The whinny of a horse outside the door of Joanna's dimly lit hut set fire to the dim embers of fear always present in Sabra's heart. She sighed. Why must their peace be interrupted? Then a knock sounded at the door and a voice called, "Is there shelter here for man and beast?"

Joanna motioned for Sabra to step into the corner behind the door. The girl stooped, gathered dirt from the earthen floor, and applied it liberally to hands, face, and arms, just as she had done the day after she returned from finding Jesus. She again tousled her hair into a black haystack and pressed her slim body against the wall of the hut.

In response to Joanna's demand to know who knocked at her door, the surprising answer nailed Sabra to her spot. Surely no one who meant harm would say in a rich, deep voice, "A shepherd of Judaea. I seek a carpenter. One called Jesus of Nazareth."

"Come in, my son." Joanna opened the door wide enough for a tall, dripping stranger to enter, yet held it so its rough surface concealed the frightened girl.

A moment later, the guest stepped back into the night to care for his horse.

"I feel in my heart we have nothing to fear from the traveler," Joanna said. "Come. We must offer him sustenance."

Pride shot through Sabra. Not one look of regret that their meager meal must be given to the stranger marred Joanna's countenance. She looked glad. Sabra silently placed an earthen bowl on the shaky table next to the last of the bread. Her belly rumbled, demanding food. The last few days she had never been filled. Both she and Joanna pretended not to be hungry and drank much water.

Sabra shrank into the shadows when the stranger came back inside carrying a wet cloak made into a bundle. He laid it down and strode to the fire, hands extended. "Peace unto you and on this house." His pleasant voice reminded Sabra of the man at the well. She muffled a laugh. The resemblance ended there. This man stood taller than most men. Rain glistened in his black, curly hair. He turned to speak to Joanna and the girl caught a glimpse of his tawny, bearded face. A good face, she decided, one that has known suffering. Compassion filled her, a shared understanding that the gods were not always kind. In what way had life wounded him, to engrave that expression in his fine, dark eyes? Regret consumed her. If Jethro had been like this traveler, she would still be in his service instead of slowly starving along with Joanna.

She flung the unworthy thought away. The dagger yet remained between her friend and starvation. Neither would she trade her encounter with Jesus, not for the finest feast Capernaum could produce. Sabra involuntarily shivered. The movement turned the stranger's gaze to where she cowered in the shadows, beyond candle stub and firelight's reach.

"I see you have a boy to help you, good mother. It is well."

Sabra's hand flew to her dirty face. She had never felt so humiliated. Masquerading as a boy to save her life and honor was one thing. To be mistaken for one by a kindly traveler sent scorching waves of shame through her body.

"It is not a boy I have, but a daughter," Joanna calmly replied. "There are those who would act unseemly should they see her as she is. Sabra, remove the earth from yourself. One who seeks Jesus of Nazareth offers no danger."

A deep flush rose to the visitor's hairline. "I — forgive my blindness." A laugh came from his strong throat. "How my father Benjamin will jeer when he learns the eyes he trained to see danger to the flocks could not discern a maiden in the shadows!" His eyes twinkled in the firelight. "Even one in — ah — such an unexpected disguise." He laughed again. "Forgive my lack of manners. I am Ara Bar-Benjamin of Bethlehem."

"You are welcome," Joanna told him. "Sit and eat."

He glanced at the single steaming bowl, at Sabra then at Joanna. "I have supplies. Perhaps you will be gracious enough to accept them in gratitude for your bread and broth." He undid the wet bundle and drew out several items. "Cheese. Dates. Dried meat. Will you not break bread with me?" He spread his cloak before the fire to dry.

Sabra longed to weep. Only the need to keep Joanna's dignity intact kept back the crowding tears. The old woman beckoned. "We thank you." She hobbled to bring two more bowls. The scant broth and vegetables would be enough for all now that they had the other food. Sabra hastily scrubbed her dirty hands, arms, and face, smoothed her hair, and took her place at the table.

Once Ara satisfied his hunger, Joanna plied him with questions. Sabra forgot to eat after the first few mouthfuls, so wonderful was Ara's story. At the old woman's urging, he began with his grandfather and father being visited by angels who came to the shepherds in the fields. Sabra felt she traveled each step the belated follower and his gray donkey Ebenezer traveled. When she learned the manger in Bethlehem lay empty on Benjamin's arrival, she flinched. What if *she* had been unable to find Him? Great danger would still surround her.

Ara at last finished the story of years past. "Father cannot leave my mother," he sadly said. "I must find Jesus and somehow bring Mother to Him so she might be healed. It is a sacred quest, given to me by my father after my wife and newborn son died." Grief filled his eyes. He shook his head and changed the subject. "I know Jesus has been here. I talked with a man at the well and another nearby, both healed by His touch."

Sabra spoke for the first time. "He also healed me."

Ara turned toward her. "*You* met Jesus?"

"Yea. He laid hands on my head. I forgot

to ask Him to straighten my arm, crooked since I was thrown down by Jethro's wicked men."

Admiration and awe registered on Ara's face before he asked, "Who is Jethro, that he should allow such a thing?" His dark brows drew into a bushy cliff and his eyes flashed.

"An advocate for the rich who steals from the poor and discredits anyone he can so he can take possession of their homes, servants, even their daughters!" Sabra cried. One hand flew to her mouth, too late to hush her angry words. What if this stranger, kind as he was, spoke of her presence with Joanna?

"Are you such a one?" he asked in his deep voice.

"You must not remember what I said, Ara Bar-Benjamin! If Jethro learns where I am it will be death for Joanna and worse for me." Revulsion filled her. She knew it showed in her face. "I beg you. Put it from your mind."

"I long to smuggle her away from Capernaum, yet fear to do so." Joanna cast a fearful glance toward the door and lowered her voice, in spite of the increasing storm that whistled and tore around the hut like a hundred spirits in torment. "Jethro watches the caravans. He has spies everywhere. Were it not that Jesus made Sabra's arm whole, she would have been discovered before now.

Jethro's hirelings seek a long-haired maiden whose arm is crooked and withered."

A triumphant smile crept to her thin lips. "The fat swine who beat on my door not long ago saw what you did this night. He went away bearing tales of a dirty-faced, ugly wench with two strong, straight arms!"

"Praise to Jehovah, I am glad he did not see what I see now, for —" Ara broke off mid-sentence. Again dull red suffused the skin visible above his dark beard.

Sabra felt an answering blush rise from the neck of her coarse garment to her forehead. She glanced down in confusion. New feelings stirred within her. The stranger had touched her heart in a way never before felt. Perhaps the sadness in his eyes, or his desire to find Jesus accounted for it. Or the strength that made her long to cast all her burdens at his muddy feet and know he would protect her and Joanna to the death. *He is only a stranger who rides away on the morrow,* an inner voice scoffed. *What has he to do with a girl pursued by Jethro? Anyone who aids a runaway is subject to danger. Should he choose to help you, it is to no avail. You dare not expose him to Jethro's wrath. It is enough that even now Joanna stands in the shadow of our master's vengeance.*

"Not *my* master," Sabra murmured so low

205

the others did not hear. Full realization had come when she looked into Jesus' eyes. Men might lay claim to her body and outward service; Jesus alone reigned over her spirit and heart.

Ara sat quietly for a long time, brow furrowed. Sabra had the feeling thoughts deep as the Sea of Galilee churned in his mind. At last he spoke. "We will talk more in the morning. There is room beside my faithful Zerah for me to sleep, if you agree."

"My shame is we have nothing better to offer you." Joanna gestured around the small room.

Ara's smile held a singular sweetness. "Fret not. Many times Zerah and I share sleeping quarters." He rose and reached for his cloak. "It is dry and warm. I bid you both a good night." He walked across the room and out the door, leaving Sabra wondering if he really had been there. She rubbed her eyes. Yea, for warmth from the broth filled her belly and a goodly store of the supplies he bestowed upon them lay on the table.

Ara's final glimpse of the woman and girl had nearly broken his heart. How could Jehovah look on such want without pain? Stay, had He not commanded men from the beginning of time to look after the weak and

206

helpless? He ran to the shed, glad the storm had abated. Zerah whinnied and nuzzled him. From his hard resting place, Ara saw a partly hidden moon peep out. It sent an off balance smile toward the drenched earth. Heavy clouds hung low, but no longer tipped their contents.

He wrapped his heavy cloak around him, warmed inside by the welcome he had received in the little hut. Before the cock crew — should anyone nearby own a cock — he must make a decision. If Jesus had gone to Passover in Jerusalem, He could be anywhere, even on His way back to Capernaum. Should he wait here for a time? Surely some from Capernaum went to Jerusalem to be filled with all that transpired. Jesus and the multitudes who followed would gain the attention of all in the city. They in turn would return to their villages with news of His doings.

Joanna and Sabra needed help. Food. Better shelter. Someone to shield them from this Jethro and his long, relentless arm. Ara's lion-like anger rose. At best, Sabra's healing and disguise offered frail protection. A single unguarded remark by anyone who knew she abided with Joanna would shatter the slender thread on which her safety hung.

How lovely she had been, once the layers

of dirt came off. Ara smiled. She reminded
him a bit of the way his wife looked the day
they wed. If he remained, she might come
to care for him. Suppose he asked for her
hand in marriage. Hot blood rushed
through him. He hadn't expected to feel
thus ever again, so deep had been his feelings for his childhood love. Now the unconscious appeal in a pair of frightened
dark eyes called to him. To stand aside and
let such a girl be taken, as he knew this
Jethro planned, was to deny his manhood.
Thanks be to God he had found her in
time. It showed in every look of her clear
eyes. Sabra's innocence wordlessly proclaimed her as yet unsullied and pure.

"It would mean delaying my quest for a
time. Surely Jehovah Himself would approve
for such a reason," he whispered to Zerah. "If
it weren't for Joanna, I could simply marry
Sabra and take her away." He considered it
and shook his head. "Nay. She will not leave
the one who took her in at such risk."

Ara finally slept but awakened un-
refreshed. He could not remember the
dreams that had troubled him. He wished he
could. They might hold a precious key to his
dilemma. By the time Sabra came out to
milk the goat, he had reached one decision,
however. "Do you think Joanna would per-

mit me to stay for a time? I can pay and mend the hut."

A lovely rose that matched the eastern sky dawned in Sabra's cheeks, far lovelier in daylight than by the dim flicker of the night before. Her clear, honest gaze met his seeking one. "It would be an answer to prayers. As you saw last night, we are starving. This day had I planned to go to the marketplace and part with my only possession." She drew the small dagger from her bosom and handed it to him, explaining its significance.

He hefted its weight in a strong hand. "This is a fine piece of work." Alarm sprang into his mind. "You must not attempt to sell it. There are those who will recognize the dagger as having belonged to your father. Joanna said Jethro had spies everywhere. They will run to him as men to the arena."

"I considered that." She gave a troubled sigh. "I care little about myself so long as I escape Jethro, but I cannot let Joanna starve. She is the only mother I remember."

A surge of desire to protect her rocked Ara. Strong man though he was, he trembled, longing to catch her close and vow to guard her with his life, if need be. *Too soon,* a little voice whispered in his soul. *Such a declaration must come later, if at all.*

Together, they went to the hut. After a

simple blessing, they partook of the remaining food. "Good mother, may I stay? I am weary with travel. So is my faithful Zerah. In return for your generosity I will go for supplies and do what I can to make your shelter more comfortable."

Joanna laid a bony, worn hand on his. "We shall be glad for the food and a strong pair of hands," she told him. "Once I would have let pride stand in my way of accepting your offer. Now I know you are sent by Jehovah, who has heard my many prayers." She paused. "What of your quest?"

Glad he had wrestled in the night with the problem, Ara said, "News will come with the return from those of Capernaum who made the long journey to Jerusalem. Until then. . . ." His shrug dismissed the importance of anything else.

A new era began in the hut. The provider skirted the city and brought stores far beyond what they could use during his stay, enough to keep them until new crops could be raised and harvested. When Joanna protested he only smiled. "You know not how great the appetite of Ara, the lion, is when he works. Now I go to earn my bread." The sound of whistling and a rain of mighty blows sang in their ears. He strengthened and enlarged the shed, making a place for himself. He made the hut so strong it could withstand storms that rocked it the way turmoil rocked the souls of men. At meals they spoke of things that troubled him. He dared not write his doubts in a message to his family and shatter their hopes, so he bided his time.

"The Roman soldier was so sure Jesus healed his centurion's servant. It causes me to wonder. How can the Messiah be the God of the Romans who prey on us as the beasts of the forest prey on those weaker?"

Joanna gently replied, "Did not Jehovah who created the rabbit also create the lion, bear, and wolf? Did he not create Romans as well as Jews?"

"It is true." Ara idly drummed his fingers on the table he had made firm. "Yea, yet I do not believe the Deliverer is for the Romans, with their many gods and vain worship of idols."

"Ara, no man can live the life of another or choose for him. You must find Jesus yourself and ask Him." She smiled, a benign look that settled his doubts for a time. "You may find when you look into His face it does not matter."

"Just as I forgot to ask for healing when I beheld him," Sabra eagerly said. Her jaggedly cut hair had grown in the time since she came to Joanna. It lay shining and curled under around her vivid face. Ara found himself unable to take his gaze from her. Even in the rough garments she continued to wear, her purity and goodness stood out like a crystal pool in a sea of mud. Both she and Joanna refused to allow their benefactor to purchase fabric.

"You do enough, my son," Joanna said. "Then, too, if either you or I were to enter a shop and make such a purchase, it would make the merchant wonder. Better for us to be clothed in sackcloth than to arouse suspicion. No one has come for a long time. I fear the day someone learns Joanna's hut is repaired and sees a fine horse in my shed."

Ara's response to that was twofold. First, he started tethering Zerah a distance behind the hut during daylight hours, sheltered by a thicket where he could not be seen. Next, he constructed a door so stout curious eyes could not peer through it. With himself sleeping behind the half-wall between his quarters and the animals, no one could enter the shed at night without his knowledge.

As time passed, the countryside hummed with rumors. Jesus, the carpenter's son from Nazareth, clearing the temple with a whip made of cords. John, the Baptizer, dead by a drunken Herod's command. Herodias, openly rejoicing over her fallen enemy and boasting how she used her daughter to inflame Herod with her lewd dancing. Gossip said John, while in prison, sent messengers to find out if Jesus was the One for whom they waited or if another would yet come. Jesus did not go to him. He sent a message referring to his healings, then praised John as the greatest prophet born of women. No one knew why He didn't save John as he had so many others.

Again, Ara wondered. Only the strong faith of Joanna, who had not seen Jesus, and Sabra, who had, offered hope to the shepherd who tarried. Duty to Joanna and his growing feelings for Sabra bound him with threads silken as his beloved's hair. How like another young couple they were! A generation earlier, Benjamin lingered with Michal until the angel of death claimed Miriam and freed her granddaughter.

thirteeen

Sabra could not point to the moment when admiration for Ara changed to another, deeper feeling. She only knew joy came in with him; his going left her bereft. What would she do when he rode away to find Jesus? Exquisite pain accompanied the thought and forced realization upon her. Ara Bar-Benjamin held her happiness in his strong, but tender, hands. She hid the knowledge in her heart, where it grew into a mighty flame, and told no one save Jehovah.

"Father, did he come only to keep us from starving?" she whispered into the night stillness long after Joanna slept. "Can it be that such a man will one day call me beloved?" Her girlish heart found it hard to believe the shepherd from Judaea watched her with more than kindly, passing interest. But the undying hope of a woman in love set her blood coursing through her veins. To be loved by Ara meant so much, not just being his wife and bearing his children. He would protect and care for her so long as she lived.

Sabra bowed her head. "According to Thy will, oh, Lord."

Recognition of her own feelings and desires made her more keenly aware of her loved one's every word or action. At times she felt as certain he loved her as that the sun would fall behind the western horizon. Other times, doubts assailed her. If he cared, as she prayed he did, why did he not speak? Sabra always answered her own unspoken question with a glance toward Joanna.

The old woman's indomitable spirit remained, but she became more and more frail. It hurt Sabra to watch her hobble about, determined to do all she could in the keeping of the household. Did Joanna not realize how fragile she had grown? A hundred times Sabra resisted the urge to speak, to tell Joanna to save her strength. She held back the words. Protesting might extend life a short time, but it would also rob the old woman of her last shreds of dignity. Better to allow her to set her own pace.

"At least I am prepared," Sabra brokenly told the little goat during a milking. "I shall miss her sorely, yet I cannot pray for her to remain. Soon she will be unable to leave her cot. Blindness is beginning to creep upon her. I see it in the way she stumbles over the little stool." She shook her head. "I cannot ask Jehovah to extend such a life. If Joanna is no longer able to be in her little garden or see the glorious sunrise, she will have no desire to live." Yet in spite of Sabra's bravery, bright tears fell against the faithful goat's side.

"Can one ever really be prepared for a visit by the angel of death?" she asked. "Nay. Joanna believes we shall meet again but doubt beats against my grieving heart like large, spattering raindrops on the roof of the hut."

The goat turned her head toward the girl who tended her.

"Do you miss her, too? Does it matter who milks and cares for you?" Sabra sighed. "You are only a goat, little friend. You cannot understand."

When Joanna smiled for the last time then closed her eyes in death, Sabra could not shed a tear. The grief inside lay too cold and heavy to permit mourning. She stared at Joanna's face, peaceful and at rest. "She — was all I had."

Ara gently laid Joanna's hand on the worn coverlet. "Nay, Sabra. You still have me, if you will honor me by becoming my wife." A poignant light came into his dark eyes. Sabra felt a mantle of peace descend over her sad heart. "I promised Joanna I would care for you."

Sabra started. Peace fled. She laid down the precious hand she still clasped then stepped back. She stared at Ara, knowing hot color rose to her cheeks. "You plan to keep your vow of duty by marrying me." Was that her frozen, lifeless voice hurling words like heavy stones out of her disappointment?

Shock sprang to his face. In a fluid movement he strode toward her and caught her hands in his. "I will keep my vow. If you wish it to be one of duty, I shall smuggle you from Capernaum, care for you as a sister, and see you safely to my father's house." His hands tightened until she wanted to cry out from the pain. "One thing you must know. The vow I made to Joanna sprang from a heart filled with love, not duty."

She sagged and would have fallen except for his hold. "Then you — care?"

"Care!" He looked into her eyes. "It has not been easy to hold my tongue, to refrain from telling you how from the moment you washed your face and I gazed into it I felt drawn to you." Honesty shone in his bearded face. "I told myself, just at first, it was because you were like the girl I married long ago. When she died, I felt never again would I feel for a woman what I once knew." Laughter set little gold flames sparkling in his eyes. "Pah! The night I came and slept with Zerah and the little goat I knew the foolishness of my belief."

The laughter died and the poignant expression returned. "Each day I watched to see if you were learning to care as I did. I found friendship in your eyes and dared to hope . . ." He drew a deep breath. "Sabra, even when I came to believe love for me lay in your heart, I could not speak because of Joanna. Only this day did I tell her, for I knew her time with us grew shorter with each hour." He took her hands again, gently this time. "Nay, I made no vow from duty, but promised to cherish and care for you always. Nevertheless, it shall be as you desire."

Sabra gave a strangled sound. Joy beyond description burst the bonds of maidenly reticence. Her musical voice filled the quiet, waiting room. "Ara Bar-Benjamin, before Jehovah, I will be your wife and bear your children, giving thanks to Him all the days of my life. The love in my heart is a deep well that can never go dry." She managed a tremulous smile.

The curly black head bowed before her.

He kissed her hands, then with a sure, deliberate motion, Ara drew her to him. His lips sought and found hers.

Sabra returned his kiss with the freshness and purity known only by those who keep themselves spotless for the mate of God's choice. She felt she had come home after a long, wandering time.

Ara released her and said huskily, "We will seek a rabbi to pronounce us one. We dare not stay here. Should others discover Joanna is dead, we would be accused of unspeakable things." He tilted her chin with one finger. Mischief filled his face and made it look boyish. "Are you willing to be a boy again for a time, just until we are husband and wife?"

Sabra grimaced at the thought. "What will be, will be. First, we must bury Joanna." Her eyes clouded. "There is nothing fitting to wrap her in save the cloak I long ago discarded for fear it would be recognized." She knelt by the cot, tears dampening her happiness.

"Joanna will glorify whatever is put on her," Ara tenderly said. "Arise, Sabra. We have much to do and little time. Prepare Joanna. I will see if I can sell the little goat." Worry wrinkled his forehead. "Are there those who will recognize her?"

"Perhaps." Sabra wiped her face. "It is best if you lead her to a faraway cottage and tie her where she can be found."

Two days later, they bid farewell to the hut and began their journey south. They must stand before a rabbi, but not in Capernaum. Would they ever return? Sabra did not know. A sharp ache filled her heart. Joanna had been so wonderful. Yet a single glance in her betrothed's face drove shadows away beneath the sunlight of his smile.

From Capernaum to Tiberias, Cana to Nazareth, stories of Jesus swirled around the tall traveler and his slight companion, dressed in boy's clothing. They had decided to be married in the village where Jesus grew up, far enough from Capernaum to attract no special attention. "Jethro would not soil his sandals or position by appearing in such a place," Sabra scoffed.

She and Ara found a multitude of persons with shining countenances and praise on their lips. All vowed that as Jesus passed by He touched them and life would never again be the same. The blind stared with open eyes. The lame leaped. The deaf listened to bird songs. The dumb shouted praises with tongues freed from silence. Each encounter confirmed the truth that Jesus was the

Messiah. They spoke of His teaching by the Sea of Galilee, of the simple prayer He gave by which the faithful could approach Jehovah as a father. They wondered aloud at Jesus' teachings to not worry over the future, to seek first the Kingdom of God and His righteousness and daily necessities would follow.

More and more Ara longed to see the One he and his father Benjamin had sought for so long. "It is not that I disbelieve your witness of Him or the miracles others proclaim," he confided to the girl at his side. "Yet I must know for myself."

He sighed. "I still find myself questioning some of the things Jesus is reported to have done. He seems to think nothing of breaking tradition. Sabra, it is said He sat down to meat in a Pharisee's house and a woman of the streets entered. She brought precious ointment, washed His feet with her tears, dried them with her long hair, kissed them, and anointed them with the costly salve!"

"What did Jesus do?"

"Simon, the host, reasoned within himself that if Jesus were a prophet He would know who and what manner of woman touched Him. Jesus discerned Simon's thoughts. He told Simon the woman's sins were forgiven; that to whom much is forgiven, the same will love much." Trouble rested in the dark eyes.

"Is it not true?" Sabra quietly asked.

"Yea, yet it causes a man to wonder." Ara shook his head. "Once I behold Jesus, I will know of a surety whether He is the Messiah. Only then can I send a message for Father to bring Mother as swiftly as he can."

Ara and Sabra pledged their love and lives to each other in Nazareth. She wore a simple gown that detracted not from her natural beauty. A handful of wildflowers picked by Ara scented the air. Sabra secretly rejoiced at being able to discard boy's clothing and teased her husband at not having recognized her maidenhood on their first meeting! When they stood alone and Ara opened his arms, Sabra flew to him like a homing pigeon to its master. Overwhelming love poured into her soul. Again, she gave thanks.

"Let us tarry for a time," Ara suggested the morning after their marriage. "We can make inquiry and discover if Jesus is expected any time soon." The mischief Sabra loved crept into his face. "Then, too, it is pleasant to be alone with my beloved wife. Once we take the road, those who also travel will intrude themselves on our happiness."

Sabra felt her color rise. Even though they had become one, she yet marveled that Ara, the lion, had joined his life with that of a runaway servant girl. He reached a long arm for her and held her close. She forgot the yesterdays and put aside thought of the tomorrows. Did they not have this day to laugh and love? Let the future bring what it would. Nothing could steal the shared joy of this moment.

A fortnight later, the world of bird songs, of sunrises and sunsets no rosier than the love that surrounded them, shattered into a thousand brittle pieces. Sabra wondered if punishment had fallen on them for tarrying in Nazareth instead of following the path toward Jesus. Ara had gone to saddle Zerah. Sabra sang while she tidied up the dwelling place they had hired for their stay in Nazareth. A slight sound in the open doorway made her turn. The greeting on her red lips died. Ara stood in the doorway, face blanched.

She ran toward him.

He held a shaking hand out, warding her off. "Touch me not, Sabra."

"Ara, what is it?" Fear smote her heart like the flat edge of a sword.

He turned his left arm over and let his wide sleeve fall back. A strange scaly patch marred its perfection, the skin surrounding it paler than the clothes Sabra washed and spread to dry in the whitening sun. "I-I discovered it when I flung the saddle on Zerah's back. It may only be a scrape, but it could be —"

"Do not speak the word!" Sabra commanded. "Such a thing cannot be." Yet a writhing serpent of dread constricted her throat until the words came out as a bare whisper. "It will heal in a day or two. We shall buy ointment from a physician, and —"

"I dare not go to a physician," Ara told her. "If he says what I feel in my heart he must say, I will be driven from Nazareth. You —" He could not go on. His dark eyes took on a hunted look. "I must get you to safety before anyone knows of this." He bowed his curly head. She saw the struggle that shook body and soul. The next instant he looked up and forced a laugh. A little color returned to his face. "It may be nothing. All we can do is to wait."

Days passed, with Sabra and Ara valiantly conquering fear for the sake of each other. He steadfastly refused to allow her to touch him in any way, despite her protests he could do her no harm. If she were to be afflicted through contact with him, surely it had already come about. He merely waved her away. By now the scaly patch had grown and another smaller spot had appeared on his leg. They could no longer deny the evidence that needed no confirmation by a physician.

"I will get you to Bethlehem," Ara promised. "There you will be welcome and safe in my father's house."

Sabra passionately demanded, "How can you think I will allow this affliction to separate us? I will follow you as Ruth followed Naomi, no matter what the outcome." She knelt before him, perfect trust in her face. "Ara, we must arise and go to Jesus immediately! I myself saw him heal a leper far more advanced than you. A single touch and the flesh of your body will grow pink with health."

"Where shall we find Him?" A thread of hope returned.

"If we do not find Him sooner, we shall meet Him in Jerusalem at Passover time. Jesus will surely be there." Yet her heart lay heavy, like a boulder loosened by tempests to plummet and rest in a hollow, empty place.

The next morning they started toward Bethlehem. "Sabra, if we do not find Him, you must promise to dwell with my family. My son Timothy and his small sister Sara need a mother. Although my sister Miriam cares for them all this long time I have searched, she has children of her own. I wish to know you are there." His lips set in a straight line and his bearded jaw set. "Neither do I wish for you to see me as I will become. Well you know what happens with lepers. When I become truly ill, I will seek the company of those like unto me. There will I find death." He looked deep into her eyes. "It shall not be farewell. Even as my father and Joanna believe that one day we shall be reunited with our loved ones, so I believe. Nay, do not protest." He raised his hand when she opened her mouth to answer. "I have prayed much. This is what must be."

Sabra said no more, though her heart beat until she felt it must burst through her chest from its heavy pounding. *Better to contract the dread disease and die with Ara than live without him,* she thought rebelliously. If he abandoned her, even to be part of his father's household, life meant nothing. She bowed her head submissively, while a frenzied prayer winged upward from her tortured heart. *Please, let us find You.*

It did not come to pass. One day Ara despondently said, "Why should I expect to find Him now, when I have not done so in all the time I have followed?"

A wellspring of knowledge came to Sabra. "Do you not see? Never before have you needed Him as you do at this moment." She drooped in the saddle, weary beyond words. She saw mist, gentle as morning dew, spring to his dark eyes, but he turned his face away from her. Sabra saw great significance in the action. Had he not begun to put her away from the second he discovered the patch on his arm?

Her foreknowledge proved accurate. Late one afternoon they stood on the crest of the hill above the valley Ara called home. He halted Zerah with a word then said, "Dismount, Sabra."

Something in his voice caused her to obey without question, her glorious strength sapped by all that had happened since she fled Jethro's household. She felt a lifetime had passed.

"I need Zerah to carry me. Go to my father. Make him believe I am dead, as Mother must be by now."

"Ara, I cannot!"

"You must. I will continue my search for Jesus. If I find Him, one day I shall return. If not — the day Zerah comes home without me is the day you will know I have again failed in my quest." His hands clenched. Great drops of sweat rose to his forehead and he brought himself under control with a visible effort. "You need not lie. When Father asks for me, simply bow your head. The tears will come." He swallowed hard. "Sabra, Father and the others must not know I am a leper. Better for them to believe I died seeking Jesus. Tell them all we have learned of Him and how no one save the Messiah could do what He has done."

"Let me go with you," she cried, hands outstretched.

He stepped back so she would not brush even the hem of his sleeve. "Nay, I shall travel faster alone."

She felt as if he had struck her in the face. Not once had she thought her presence hampered, slowed him down. Anger flared, crumpled, died in the face of his misery. "Peace unto you, my beloved," she whispered. One hand stole to her breast and seized the precious dagger. "Sell this. You will have need of the money it brings."

Ara silently accepted it and slipped it into his tunic, carefully avoiding the slightest touch of her slender hand.

"Make haste to find Jesus. He can heal you." Sabra crossed her arms over her aching heart, clung to her faith, and watched Ara lead Zerah back over the hilltop. He did not look back. She sensed he dared not linger lest he be tempted to stay.

When her keen ears could no longer detect footsteps of man or beast, Sabra turned her face to the valley below and slowly started down the rolling hill into a new life.

Ara thought he had known pain when his wife and child died. Now it intensified until it threatened to drive him mad. "We must find Jesus," he told Zerah. "Will He heal me, as He has healed others?" If only he had the faith Sabra, child of betrayal, possessed! Memory of his last sight of her haunted him day and night. It rose between him and the dusty road he often thought went nowhere. It gleamed in the fire's glow when he made his evening meal. A dozen times when he felt he must give up the quest, find a cave or hole in the rocks as wounded beasts do, Sabra's clear glance made him doggedly keep on. He followed every stray piece of information on Jesus' whereabouts, wandered the land until his clothing grew tattered.

One morning, Zerah lifted his head and faced toward Bethlehem. He whinnied. A pang went through Ara. Why must the faithful companion suffer along with his master? His promise to Sabra rang in the clear air.

The day Zerah comes home without me is the day you will know I have failed in my quest.

"I will take you home, good friend," he promised. "I shall look once more on the land of my birth, perhaps catch a glimpse of Sabra or Father, Timothy or Sara. Then I shall go away to die." He fought back the weakness accompanying his spreading illness, mounted Zerah and started over the long, tedious miles toward home.

fourteen

"Zerah, if I do not find Jesus, this will be my last pilgrimage." Ara's face twisted in pain. Never again would he ride through the hills and valleys he loved so much. Never would he gaze into the faces of those he loved or hear Zerah whinny a morning greeting. Once he freed the black, his companions would be the living dead.

If only he could ride openly into the valley and behold the family who longed for his return! Ara's lips whitened. His jaw set and he shook his head. His growing weakness warned how near the death angel stood at his elbow. He proudly lifted his haggard face to the murky sky. "So be it. I will not endanger my loved ones by coming into their presence. Neither will I die in their midst like a sniveling coward. Nay. I have tasted life at its sweetest. Now I drink the bitter dregs, but I will die like a man."

Ara reached the final valley and paused. The saddle must not be warm when Zerah arrived without him. He halted until even Benjamin could not guess how recently the black had carried a rider. At last he struggled up the last hill, panting from the exertion. The journey home had taken a heavy toll.

Morning mists swirled around the crest. Zerah's pace quickened. He pranced a bit in spite of his obvious weariness. Ara patted the dusty black neck. "No sadness in this coming home for you, my friend."

They paused at the crest of the hill. The valley lay at their feet, wisped with fog, thick with sheep and — "Timothy, my son," Ara whispered. He stared at the lad who lay sleeping a few rods away. The first light of day fell on the upturned face that showed signs of manliness in its youth. Did the drooping lips come from loneliness for his father? One brown hand firmly clasped a cudgel. Ara smiled, remembering how he, too, fought sleep while keeping watch over the sheep. The smile faded. He must take care. The slightest sound could rouse a shepherd.

Heart thumping from the unexpected encounter. Ara dismounted and whispered in Zerah's ear, "Go home."

The horse didn't move.

"Go home, I tell you!" For the first time, Ara struck his horse, then ran to the shelter of a nearby bush. With a startled whinny, Zerah sprang forward.

The next instant, Timothy stood rubbing sleep from his dark eyes. Before his father's watching eyes, youth fled from his face until he looked like an old man. Had he not then accepted the death of his father? Had the coming of the riderless Zerah forced him to recognize it? A hoofbeat later, Timothy raced after the black. His childish cry reached the ears of the man crouching in the frail protection of a bush. "Zerah?"

Why did I come? Ara censured himself, even while he bent low and took advantage of Timothy's concentration on the black. The lad might return at any moment. He must find better cover. A larger bush offered it. Ara burrowed into it, barely aware of reaching thorns that snagged his tattered cloak and clawed hands, face, and arms. 'Curling into the smallest possible ball, he bit the inside of his cheeks until he tasted sickish blood. Timothy must not find him here. From the depths of the bush, he cautiously peered out.

Timothy's call had stopped Zerah. The lad caught him by his worn bridle and buried his face in the tangled mane, then he raised his voice in a mighty cry that tore at Ara's heart and left it bleeding even more than the wounds from the thorny hiding place. "Grandfather, Zerah has come back."

Ara's body responded to the cry his mind said he must disregard. Only the clutching thorns kept him from casting caution to the winds. Before he could free himself, reason prevailed. *Nay! To let them see you so then go away means dying not once, but twice. Ara Bar-Benjamin, you cannot do this, for Timothy's sake, for Sabra's and the others'.* Ara sagged. Manhood returned. He had charted his course. A moment of weakness must not undo what he had coldly planned while in control.

Ara did not see the sun climb high in the heavens and later set in a burst of glory. He lay half-unconscious, afraid to move for fear of detection. Only when the pitiless stars came out and peered down did he rouse. The night wind he once loved now hurled taunts at him. He did not belong here. He must go. Before dawn, Ara slipped from his shelter and stumbled away without a backwards glance. In his weakened condition, he did not trust himself, should he behold Timothy or one of the others.

★★★

Ara, the leper, trudged highways and byways, seeking Jesus. His worn sandals gave out. He mended them with pieces of his garments. They turned to rags and he walked barefoot, too proud to beg of those whose fine horses and chariots passed him by. His feverish mind seized on a gruesome thought with horrid fascination. Why not ask a physician to cut off the diseased arm, the patch on his leg? It obsessed him until the day he wiped his sweaty face and realized patches had spread to face and neck.

Creeping horror left him paralyzed. "God of Abraham, Isaac, and Jacob, why tormentest Thou me? Grant me mercy, I beseech Thee!" It came out as a whisper. Ara tottered to the side of the road and collapsed, the dream of reaching Jesus deader than all the prophets who had gone before. Troubled dreams haunted him. Unanswered questions. Surely Benjamin had sought his son when no messages came. Why had he not found him? Or had he been unable to leave Mother? Did she still live? Had Sabra obeyed his last request and led them to believe their son dead, as he soon would be? How could Jehovah look on the world's suffering and yet send His Son to be part of it? Was Jesus the Promised One, the

Messiah? At that point, Ara's mind balked. He fell into a welcome stupor and knew no more.

It took every ounce of strength and courage Sabra possessed to walk down the hillside and into Benjamin Bar-Ara's presence. He stood outside his home, waiting for her to reach him.

"Lad, you are out early." He smiled and she saw how Ara would look if permitted to live to his father's age.

She felt herself flush. "I-I am not a lad but a woman." She removed her headcovering and stood before him. "The roads are unsafe for women."

Amazement filled his dark eyes even as he said, "Welcome to my house, daughter. Have you traveled far? Why are you alone? Have you no husband to protect you?"

The words stuck in her throat. Sabra had to pry each one loose, sorting them with care. "I had a husband." She felt her face pale and twist with pain. Tears gushed, as Ara had predicted. She bowed her head and brokenly added. "You speak more truly than you know when you call me daughter."

The still-powerful shepherd's frame jerked. "You — are — was Ara. . . ?"

She silently nodded and clasped her hands before her.

A gnarled hand rested on her hair. "Come, child, for you are little more than that. I will take you to Michal."

"She is yet alive? Ara feared she had died."

"Alive and healed by the power of the Almighty, praise His name!" Benjamin's voice rolled out. Yet Sabra sensed his pain, his questions.

Father, give me the words to say, she prayed.

No mighty rush of wind followed. No voice spoke from heaven. Yet when she told of Ara's quest, Joanna's goodness, and her own healing from Jesus, strength filled her. Sabra purposely did not give times when this or that happened. When they asked about Ara's death, she held out her arms in pleading. "Forgive me. I cannot bear to speak of it. He bade me come to you when he could no longer be with me." Every word the truth, yet she felt they must see through her dissembling and know the monstrous lie she allowed them to believe. If Ara found Jesus, one day they would understand and forgive.

"You will dwell here," Michal said. As simply as that, Sabra found a home.

Young Timothy pushed close. "Where is my father's horse Zerah?"

Sabra felt cold sweat dampen her back. "I know not."

"Why did you not ride him on your journey to us? Did you sell him?"

She could only helplessly shake her head and turn her gaze away from Timothy's demanding dark eyes that reminded her of his father.

"Enough questioning, Timothy." Benjamin rose, shoulders bowed with grief. "We shall speak of it no more."

What have I done? Sabra flayed herself. *Why must I be the one to destroy hope, to bring sadness to this family? Yet if they knew their son wandered the land as a leper, would their hearts not ache far more?* Compassion overrode guilt and brought a measure of peace.

Within a few short days, Sabra felt she had lived near Bethlehem since childhood. At times her former life took on the semblance of a dream. Benjamin and Miriam's husband hastily built a small cottage for Sabra and Ara's children. She had haltingly told the family Ara's last wish had been for her to love and care for Timothy and Sara. She rejoiced when Timothy took his sister by the hand and said, "This is the new mother Father sent. Sara, you must help her as you did Miriam. I will care for you both, as Father would. I am almost a man." He blinked hard.

She longed to fling her arms around the boy and tell him to weep away the pain in his eyes. She wisely refrained. "I shall be glad for your care, Timothy. Sara, I know you will be of much help to me."

More and more dreamlike the past grew, although the constant aching for her husband remained. She fiercely clung to the hope he would find Jesus and be healed. That hope blossomed brighter than ever when she realized Jehovah had blessed her greatly. "If, nay, *when* Ara returns, how glad he will be to know I carry his child," she whispered, keeping her secret close in her heart for a time.

Yet the glow that surrounded her betrayed Sabra. When Michal quietly asked, the young wife nodded, too filled with joy to speak.

"I will care for my brother," Timothy stated. He grew taller with each passing day, thoughtful and considerate of Sabra at all times.

Sabra's eyes twinkled. "Perhaps Jehovah will send a girl."

"Then Sara shall help care for her." Timothy grinned. "But I shall still love her as I do this one." He patted his sister's head.

"No babe could ever have a better brother and sister," Sabra told him and Sara. "I want you to know, I shall not love the new one any more than I love you. You are part of Ara and because of it, we are also one."

"I wish my father had not died." Sara laid her head on Sabra's shoulder. "He was gone so long, sometimes it is hard for me to remember what he looked like," she for-lornly added.

Timothy scoffed at the idea, yet Sabra caught a flash of fear in his dark eyes. "Ara looked much like Benjamin, only younger. He also looked much like Timothy, only older."

Sara giggled. It brought an answering smile to her brother's face, but a few days later Sabra arose early and found the lad missing from their little home. Strange. Day had barely dawned. Had he slipped out to be among the sheep in the night hours, as he sometimes did? She stepped to the doorway and squinted, the better to see through the fog. Where could he be? For all Timothy's boasting of manhood, he was yet a little boy. Should she call his name or search for him among the quiet sheep?

Sabra shook her head. Doing so would be a blow to his dignity. He tried so hard to take his father's place. Not by word or action could she allow him to feel he had failed.

A commotion on the hillside above caught her attention. A sharp sound carried to her through the clear air. The neigh of a horse. Drumming hoofbeats. A dusty black horse running toward her. Sabra felt the blood drain from her heart. *The day Zerah comes home without me is the day you will know I have failed in my quest.* The words shouted in her ears, clear as the treble call that came next.

"Zerah?" Timothy burst out of the fog, reached the black. "Grandfather, Zerah has come back," he screamed.

People spilled from doorways. Sabra stood frozen. Unless he lay dying, Ara would never have sent Zerah home.

"How could he come?" Timothy wondered. "See, he is weary. He must have come far." The boy laid his cheek on the heaving side. "Perhaps he escaped from thieves. He still bears his saddle but it is cold." He sighed. "We will never know." Timothy straightened. "Zerah is mine now." He walked away, leading the tired horse. The look in his face showed the boy Timothy had vanished forever, replaced by one who claimed his father's horse as his birthright.

Winter gave way to spring, bringing plans to go to Jerusalem. "All my life I was too late," Benjamin said sadly. "I fear if we do not see Jesus this Passover, we never shall. Rumors of plotting against Him trouble me. It is said secret meetings of the high priests and Pharisees increase all the time. News has it Jesus no longer walks openly among the Jews, not since he raised Lazarus from the dead. He may not even come to the Passover."

Some of the strain left Benjamin's face. "I myself talked with a good man who saw it happen. Jesus must be the Messiah. No other could call forth a man from his grave. Is it any wonder His enemies hate Him? The Roman emperor thinks he is divine. Pah." The corners of his mouth turned down. "All he can do is to send people to their death. Jesus conquered death. Who can imagine all that it means?"

Timothy stood before his grandfather, clenched fists on the hips of his tunic. "I shall not go to the Passover," he stated. "Jehovah let my father die."

In vain the women pleaded with him.

"Nay. I stay with the sheep," Timothy insisted.

"I am thankful, my son," Sabra quietly

said. She laughed. "The little one kicks until I am weary. I will be glad when the next weeks pass and the child is born. You and I and Sara shall remain while the others go."

Suspicion showed in the way the boy's eyes narrowed to slits. "Think you not I can care for the sheep alone? Did not my grandfather stay behind when the other shepherds went to see the baby in Bethlehem?"

"He missed the Christ-child. Would you, too, miss the Messiah?" Sara demanded. "Mother, can I not go with the others?" Disappointment swept into her sweet face.

Sabra saw the struggle in Timothy's eyes, the twinge of regret. He had told her many times how he loved the Passover: the beautiful temple, the other children, the solemn reading of the holy scriptures. "Sara must go. I will stay. And you, Mother, if you are not well."

"What if you have need of help?" Benjamin asked, brows knitting into a straight line above his keen eyes.

Timothy flashed a smile. "Zerah is strong. He could carry Mother to safety."

"And you?"

"I will be with the sheep. A good shepherd does not leave his flock."

Sabra averted her face to keep from laughing, as much at the pride in Benjamin's eyes as the self-proclaimed sheep protector's boasting!

Michal drew Sabra aside when all but Timothy had gone to prepare for their journey. Worry showed in her face. "Are you truly ill, daughter? I shall not leave you if you need me."

Sabra shook her head. "Nay. You must go. The babe will not come until after you return. I will have need of you then. For now, Timothy will care for me." She exchanged understanding smiles with Michal and beamed on Timothy. He swelled with importance.

Deep in her heart, Sabra hid her longing to again see the temple. She knew by the look in Timothy's eyes he felt the same but would not admit such weakness. The small caravan wound up, over the hill and out of sight, leaving the two to keep the sheep.

The day after the others left, restlessness left Sabra unable to stick with any one task for long. "How far away are our nearest neighbors?" she inquired. "I do not remember hearing."

"There are other shepherds in distant fields," Timothy loftily said. "They are too old and uncaring to seek a messiah."

"Are there women among them?"

He shook his head. "I cannot say. I do not remember seeing any when we sought a sheep that strayed. Usually they stay in our valley or on the hillsides unless we drive them elsewhere. Why do you ask?" He cocked his head to one side and surveyed her with shining eyes.

Sabra laughed uneasily. "I know not," she admitted. One hand lay on her swollen belly. "The babe kicks hard this day." She hesitated and forced herself to add in a calm tone, "Timothy, have you watched — helped — at lambing time?"

He snorted disdainfully. "Yea, ever since I was a child." Excitement filled his eyes. "It is a wondrous thing how Jehovah prepared a place for the lamb to hide and grow until time to be born."

She smiled and told him, "How good it is you have this knowledge! Why, if the others should be delayed in returning from Jerusalem, and if your brother or sister decided to come to us early, you could help me as you did the lambs." Sabra looked deeply into his dark eyes, trying to give him a sense of confidence. Could a child his age assist her should her babe come early?

"I think so." He gulped. "Mother, it will not happen like that, will it? Shall I mount Zerah and ride like the wind? Zerah can easily overtake the caravan; they move slowly. He is strong and can carry both Grandmother and me on our return journey. I am sure you and the sheep will be safe for the short time I am gone." Eagerness and flecks of fear danced in his eyes.

She thought for a moment. Surely the qualms that began the moment the travelers vanished over the hilltop were foolish. She had carefully figured the time. Her child should be born some time after the Passover-bound pilgrims returned. Why spoil their pleasure and hamper Benjamin in his delayed search? He would turn back with Michal, should Timothy go for her.

"I am merely curious." Sabra patted Timothy's hand. "It also brings me peace to know how well cared for I am."

He reddened and announced, "I must go see to the sheep."

Sabra watched her small protector through the open doorway. Such a sturdy replica of Ara! His cheerful whistle secretly comforted her. The capable hands that had helped bring lambs into the world might tremble if called on to perform a far different task. Yet she knew Timothy Bar-Ara would do his best. He stood between her and the terror of delivering her baby alone, should the child come unexpectedly.

fifteen

Sickness, hunger, and fading hope left Ara in a huddled heap. He cared nothing for those who passed. Even the scornful jeers that once would have roused black anger went unheeded. What did it matter? He had searched for Jesus and failed to find Him.

The thrum of hoofbeats pierced Ara's apathy, followed by the command, "Halt!" Heavy, booted feet tramped toward him. He looked up, into a Roman centurion's face. "Arise and be gone, Jewish dog!" the man ordered. "Lepers do not belong beside the roads Romans travel."

Too weak to argue, Ara stumbled away. He reached a clump of concealing bushes before he fell next to a stunted tree. The creak of leather and neigh of horses told him the company had dismounted for a rest. He knew no fear. They could not see him. Neither would they come close enough to risk being touched by a leper. Ara crouched behind the tree, legs shaky, breath coming hard. He could hear every word of their coarse talk. He tried to shut it out, but his ears opened wide when he heard the name Jesus.

"What say you of Jesus?" the centurion rumbled in his throat. "Even some of our comrades have felt the man's bewitching power."

"If it is true Jesus raised a man from the dead, then —"

"Foolishness! If even the emperor cannot do such a thing, how can a carpenter from Nazareth have power over death?"

"I don't know." A brief silence fell. "I do know one cannot travel to any part of Galilee, Samaria, or Judaea without hearing wild tales of the one called Jesus." Ara heard a wistful note in the speaker's voice. "I am almost tempted to seek the man out and see for myself."

"Pah! Jesus is an impostor who will soon be hanged on a tree like a hundred others who incur the wrath of those in power. Come. We must not tarry longer. The sun hangs low."

"Where is Jesus, anyway?"

Ara recognized the voice of the man who confessed himself tempted to find Jesus.

A rude laugh came. "By Jupiter, Mercury, and Mars, that is what the high priests and Pharisees wish to know. Some say the carpenter is in Ephraim. Who cares? If they find Jesus it means another crucifixion. How I hate them! Thank the gods such punishment is reserved for the commonest of criminals."

A murmur of assent swelled through the soldiers.

Ara barely heard them ride away. So Jesus had raised a man from the dead. The afflicted man's face contorted. He wished he had not heard the Romans' idle talk. He had resigned himself to death. Now an ember he believed dead flickered into pale life. Go to Ephraim, it whispered.

His laugh sounded loud in the stillness. How could a man barely able to get out of the Romans' way travel even the few miles that stretched between him and Ephraim? Yet the relentless whisper pounded into his brain until he felt he must obey or be driven mad with its steady beat.

If Ara lived until the sun, moon, and stars vanished, he would never forget how he struggled to reach Ephraim. Night followed day and blended into a sea of wretchedness. Sometimes he walked, bent and disease-ridden. When he could walk no longer, he crawled — a miserable heap of slow-moving rags. Somehow he reached a pile of rocks not far from his destination. "So close and yet so far," he sobbed. Not even for the Messiah could he go one more step. He cast himself on the ground.

"If I could only catch one glimpse of Him before I die," he gasped. "Father in heaven, must I leave this world never knowing if Jesus is the Messiah?" Only the distant cry of a night-prowling beast answered. Close to death, Ara fell asleep. All night long he lay on his harsh bed of rocks, too exhausted to care.

He awakened and felt the warmth of the sun. The next moment it was blotted out. Something or someone stood between him and the rising sun. Ara cringed. If the centurion who ordered him away from the road found him here, it meant a lashing. If the man were a Jewish priest, Ara would fare little better. Severe punishment awaited lepers who trod in places except the caves and hovels to which they were banished at the first sign of sickness.

Ara sighed. *Pah, what does it matter?* He would never see Jesus. Perhaps Jehovah had not even heard the faint prayer of a condemned man. Why should he grovel in these final moments of life? With his last measure of strength, he defiantly raised his head. A man stood etched against sunlight so brilliant Ara could not discern his features. His shadow spread over Ara's prone body.

"Who are you and what do you want with a hopeless leper?" Ara croaked. Before the words left his mouth, every muscle, sinew, and bone wrenched. He felt himself being pulled apart. He hadn't known dying could be such a terrible thing. "God, be merciful to me, a sinner!" burst from parched lips.

The agony continued. A minute or an eternity later his vision cleared. He again beheld the man surrounded by light, only this time he discerned kind eyes in a bearded face — and knew. "Jesus. Messiah."

One hand descended to touch Ara's shoulder. A voice bade him to rise and be made whole. He awkwardly got to his knees, then stood on shaking legs, ignoring the rending of body that still sent spasms throughout him. Gradually, they stilled. Ara raised both arms toward Jesus. His ragged sleeves fell back. The arm that had shrunken to little more than bone with tautly stretched skin was no longer leprous.

He stared, then tore the clothes from his body until he stood clothed in only a frayed loincloth. No sign of the dreaded disease remained.

"I am free! Praise God!" Ara fell to his knees and reached out to touch the hem of Jesus' robe. His fingers closed on emptiness. He looked up. Nothing stood between him and the radiant sun. He rubbed his eyes. Had it all been a dream? Nay, for beneath the soil of travel, his body showed well and strong.

"I did not find Him." Ara ran one hand over his dazed face. "He found me and made me well." He leaped into the air like a madman, kicked his bare heels together, shouted praises until they echoed between distant hills. Then he ran until his lungs felt they would burst. "I must show myself to the priests, even though I know what they will say."

"We find no sign of uncleanness in you," they told him after their examination. "Do you know of a surety you were leprous?"

"I know. Jesus healed me, I tell you." For a moment he felt they would revise their verdict. They dared not, although black hatred crept into their eyes. An hour later, he started for home. What cared he that he had not eaten properly for days? Not only had the leprosy vanished, but Ara's superb strength came back with such vigor he strode the dusty roads like a king in tattered clothing.

Straight for his father's house near Bethlehem he headed, resenting the crowds that swarmed the roads. "Ah, Passover," he murmured. "We shall go, all of us." He considered. "I can get there more quickly if I travel the byways." He turned aside to a less used path, not knowing his doing so caused him to miss his family, already on the way to Jerusalem.

At last he stood on the crest of the hill, blinded by tears. Below him lay everything he had turned away from long ago. Late, slanting sunlight cast a golden haze over the valley. Soon night would fall. Ara impatiently brushed away the film before his eyes and started down the hillside. A black horse glanced up from where he grazed, hesitated, then loped toward the shabby figure. His shrill neigh split the peaceful valley air.

"Zerah!" Ara raced to meet him, a smile curling his lips. Surely the sound would bring his family to the doorway.

No one appeared.

"Where are they, old friend?" He stroked Zerah's neck, noticing how well kept and fat the horse had grown. "Surely they would not go away and leave you." He sprang to the black's back and urged him into a run. A thin wail came from a house that not been there when he brought Sabra. Fear attacked.

Ara halted Zerah beside the house, leaped down, and stepped inside, blinking to adjust his sight from the bright outdoors to the more dimly lit room.

The morning Jesus healed Ara, Sabra had realized her baby would not wait until the family returned. "Timothy," she said, trying to keep her voice calm and not frighten him. "I believe we shall have a visitor today."

"A visitor?" Quick understanding leaped to his eyes. "You mean —"

"Your little brother or sister will not delay coming," Sabra told him. "I shall need your help." A spasm of pain caught her and she waited until it passed. "We must have hot water and a sharp knife to sever the cord that binds the baby to me. You must warm swaddling clothes; they are prepared and ready. You will also need to warm olive oil."

Timothy's eyes rounded. "I could ride Zerah and see if there are women in the other fields."

"Nay, there is no time. You can do everything I cannot, my son. It is not so different from lambing time." She sent silent prayers toward heaven that her travail might be short. She prayed for courage and strength. She beseeched Jehovah to take away Timothy's fear and her own.

254

Sabra's prayers were heard and answered. Before the sun reached the top of the sky, a lusty man-child squalled his way into the world. During the delivery, Timothy's face had been white and pinched. The moment the baby slid into his waiting hands, color returned to his cheeks. He oiled and wrapped the infant and laid it in Sabra's eager arms.

"Did I do everything right?" he asked.

Tears spilled. "My son, no one could have done better." Sabra sniffled. "Isn't he beautiful?"

Timothy thought for a long moment. "He is very small, but he will grow. His name must be Ara, for the father he will never know." The boy's lips trembled for the first time during the ordeal.

"Little Ara. You have chosen well, my son." Her clasp tightened on the wrapped bundle. Sadness intruded in her moment of fulfillment. Surely Ara must be dead. Many weeks had passed since Zerah returned. Ara never even knew he was to have a son.

Did Timothy divine her thoughts? Perhaps, for he said, "We will teach him to be strong and tall. I shall take him into the fields and teach him to care for the sheep and lambs. Mother —" He broke off, then fixed his questioning gaze on Sabra. "Do you think Father would want me to give Zerah to Ara, when he is old enough?"

Sabra sensed what it took for him to offer. She emphatically shook her head. "Nay. You are the firstborn son, Timothy. Zerah is yours. One day you shall lift Ara to the horse's back and teach him to ride, but he must have a different horse, not Zerah."

Timothy grinned in obvious relief. He faithfully sat beside Sabra while she slept for a time. He brought food when she roused, almost bursting with the pride of being man of the household. The day wore on, quiet and peaceful. Now and then Timothy went outside to make sure no harm had befallen the sheep. He always returned, fascinated by his small brother.

"Is he sick or angry?" he asked when the baby awakened and wailed.

"Nay. He is hungry." She turned him toward the source of food.

"As am I. Have you food and shelter for a wandering beggar?" a voice asked from the doorway.

Sabra looked up. "Ara?" She closed her eyes, opened them again.

Timothy looked as if he had seen a spirit. "Father?"

"You're alive and well!" Sabra struggled to a sitting position, babe still at her breast.

"Oh, Ara!" The world of pain and loss she had experienced echoed in those two, poignant words.

Timothy came out of his trance. He flung himself into his father's arms. "You aren't dead! Father, where have you been this long, long time? We missed you so!" The bravery he had shown in Sabra's hour of need fled. Again the little boy he should be, Timothy huddled in his father's strong arms and cried out all the sadness of the last many months.

"Sabra, what — who — ?" Ara picked Timothy up and strode to the bed, child in his arms. "A baby?"

"Our son. His name is Ara, after his father and great-grandfather." She could hardly believe her husband had come back. "You are well and strong," she repeated. "How can such a thing be?"

"Jesus healed me." Ara gently touched the baby with one exploring finger.

"Were you very ill, Father?" Timothy clung like a leech, as if fearful Ara would vanish should he let him go.

"Unto the death. The leprosy had —"

"Leprosy!" Timothy stiffened at the frightening word.

"Yea. That is why I sent Sabra to be your mother, so you could care for her as I no longer could."

"He has truly fulfilled all you yourself would have done for me," Sabra praised. She rejoiced at the pride in both pairs of matching dark eyes and added, "In fact, he may have done better in helping bring little Ara. You were always more of a carpenter than a shepherd!"

Ara laughed and looked around. "Where are the others? Did Miriam not know you would have need of her? Why did you not go to Jerusalem?"

Sabra caught the look of appeal Timothy sent to her. "I did not feel well when they left. Timothy stayed with me. The babe came far earlier than expected. Benjamin, Michal, Miriam, and the others had no way of knowing what would happen in their absence."

"Michal! Then Mother is alive?" Ara unceremoniously set Timothy on his feet. "I must take her to Jesus. I know He will heal her."

"Grandmother was made well by the hand of God long ago," Timothy piped up. "She sings at her work." A shadow crossed his expressive face. "At least she did before Sabra came and then Zerah."

"Is this true?" Ara whipped around toward Sabra.

"Yea." Sabra valiantly conquered the

desire to beg Ara to stay with her. "Make haste and go to Jerusalem. She and Benjamin, Sara, Miriam, and the others must wait no longer to learn the wonderful thing that has happened."

"You ask me to leave you?" Ara marveled. "Sabra, how can I go?" The anguish he had experienced while they were apart showed more in his tone than words conveyed.

"Have you forgotten my protector so soon?" She laughed through bright tears. "Timothy, I know you long to go to Passover with your father, but I need you. Will you stay?"

He came to her bedside and laid one stubby hand on the coverlet. Relinquishment of a dream showed in his face, along with determination. "Go, Father. I will care for my mother."

"You are a son to make a man's heart glad," Ara huskily said. "Can you find me other clothing? These garments are disgraceful and fit only to be burned." Timothy ran out and his father turned to Sabra. He gathered her and their child into his strong arms. "Never can you know what I have lived through."

Her woman's heart rose to argue, but Sabra's lips kept silent. One day they would speak of many things. Not now. Ara must hasten to Jerusalem at first light and already dusk crept into the valley. She saw beyond his excitement and realized he needed food and rest. If only she could minister to him! Soon, her heart promised. The rest of their lives spread out ahead of them.

Bathed, fed, and clothed in tunic and robe he had left behind so long ago, Ara bore little resemblance to the haggard man who brought Sabra to Bethlehem. The next morning he solemnly asked if he could borrow Zerah and rode away. Timothy waved him out of sight and came back into the house. "Jehovah is good. Mother, why did you allow us to think Father dead?"

"I could not deny what might be his last wish." She drew in a troubled breath. "He felt if you knew he lived as a leper, you could not bear the pain as I have done." A quick sob escaped her. "He is well now. We can put sadness aside and rejoice. Oh, but it will be wonderful when they all return. How glad they will be you cared for me so well, my son."

Swift as night Zerah covered the miles to Jerusalem. How good it felt to sit on his back! Ara talked with him as before. The black's ears pricked up and he held his head high, prancing when Ara loosened the reins.

When they arrived, it took time to find those they sought. Ara and Zerah worked their way past a multitude of camps until Ara spotted his family apart from the throng. He halted his mount. He must get control of himself before going to them. His gaze rested first on his mother. Why, she looked younger and stronger than she had the day he rode away to find Jesus! Her lips curled upwards in a sweet smile as she stroked Sara's head. How his daughter and the other children had grown. Miriam and her husband had changed little.

Benjamin stood to one side. He, too, looked much the same except for his ever-whitening hair and furrowed face. The keen eyes under his roof of white eyebrows held a far-seeing look.

Would the arrival of one they thought dead bring ill effects? Should he send Zerah ahead, to prepare them? Nay. They would think something had happened to Timothy or Sabra.

He could delay no longer. He slid from Zerah's back and walked out of the shadows into the circle of light made by one of a thousand cooking fires. "Father, it is Ara."

The figures around the fire stood as though transfixed. Every vestige of color fled their faces. Mouths hung open, but no voices came. Michal shook off the bonds of disbelief first. She sprang to meet her tall son. "Ara, child of my body!" The fierceness of her clasp around his waist showed how truly she had been made whole.

Benjamin leaped toward them. "My son, my son, how can it be? All this time . . ." He could not continue. "Why did Sabra not tell us you lived?"

"She knew not at what moment I would die. She only knew leprosy had come to me. I forbade her to tell you. Better that you believed me dead. She sent me to find Jesus. I tried, so hard. When I had given up hope of finding Him, He came to me. Father, He is the Messiah."

Ara freed an arm and gripped his father's hand. Benjamin responded by gathering both him and Michal into a mighty embrace. "My son who was as dead now lives. Let us give thanks."

With one accord, they fell to their knees. Benjamin's voice rolled out like the patriarch he was, in a paean of praise to the One who had restored his only son. The stars shone upon them, foretelling a fair day on the morrow — a day when all the world should know the greatness of God and rejoice.

sixteen

For thirty-three years Benjamin had sought the Messiah and, now, he found Him on a cross beneath a sign that bore the inscription: JESUS OF NAZARETH, THE KING OF THE JEWS. A thief hung on either side of him, cursing and groaning. Roman soldiers cast lots at the foot of the three crosses.

"My eyes betray me," the old shepherd brokenly told his trembling wife. "Did we not hear the multitude shouting praises when Jesus rode into the city on the colt? They waved branches from the palm trees to welcome Him." Great cords stood out on his neck. "Surely Jehovah will smite those who have done this hideous thing. I am glad Miriam, her family, and Sara stayed at our camp and that Timothy, Sabra, and the newborn child are safe at home."

Ara spoke from behind them. "Judas Iscariot betrayed Jesus with a kiss, for thirty pieces of silver. The Promised One's disciples ran away when the soldiers came to arrest Him in the Garden of Gethsemane where He prayed. It is whispered the Master prophesied Simon Peter would deny Him thrice before the cock crowed. Peter swore to be true, yet it came to pass."

"Surely Caiaphas and the high priests know they have condemned an innocent man." Michal leaned against Benjamin's strong arm and wept. "Even Pilate said he found no fault in Jesus."

"Pah!" Benjamin spat. "Pilate is a Roman dog, afraid of losing his position. Every person in Jerusalem knows he could have saved Jesus. Nay. He dared not go against the crowd when they cried for the release of the robber Barabbas." He could not tear his gaze from the sickening scene above him.

"If only the high priests had accepted the coins we have hoarded so long as a purchase price for Jesus' freedom," Michal whispered. To speak of gold in the maddened throng was to invite danger. Hot-eyed men with greedy faces darted through the multitude, taking advantage of the milling people to ply their thieving trade without detection.

In horrid fascination, the family from Bethlehem remained — watching, praying, hoping Jesus would save Himself, as He had saved others. Once he prayed, "Father, forgive them: for they know not what they do."

Benjamin marveled. Hatred rose and left him shaken. Why did Jesus not call down fire from heaven to destroy His enemies? A strange darkness fell over the land about the sixth hour, as though the sun could not bear to shine even in the middle of the day. Rumors spread through the crowd that the veil of the temple had been rent in twain from top to bottom. Spectators, frightened by the terrible blackness, ran from the hill and sought refuge in their homes.

Benjamin, Ara, and Michal remained. "Surely He will yet save Himself," Michal murmured. "We must be here."

Her prayers went unanswered. At about the ninth hour Jesus cried out, "It is finished." His matted head with its crown of thorns bowed to His breast. He moved no more.

In despair, Benjamin fell to the ground. Jesus had raised Lazarus from the dead yet allowed Himself to be crucified. Why? The belated follower beat the earth with his fists. As if in answer, the heavens spoke with a fury seldom seen. Weeping and wailing, bystanders fled. The Roman soldiers had long since parted Jesus' raiment. The centurion in charge who stood over Him proclaimed, "Truly this man was the Son of God."

Benjamin's hatred left him. The Roman soldiers had only been doing their duty. Jesus' death must be laid where it belonged at the feet of the high priest Caiaphas and his cohorts. Had Jesus begged forgiveness from His Father in heaven on behalf of the soldiers? Benjamin shook his head, too weary to ponder it. Ara's strong arm lifted him to his feet.

"Come, Father. We can do no more." Grief furrowed his face. With a final backwards glance toward the little group of women who lingered, they turned their steps toward the encampment.

"His poor mother," Michal sobbed. "One who stood near me said she saw the whole thing." Her body shook.

"He spoke truly," Benjamin said, voice lifeless. "It is finished." Why did invisible wings brush his heart when he remembered the centurion's cry? It caused him to say, "I am weary. I will remain in Jerusalem for a few days beyond the Sabbath. Ara, will you stay?"

"Nay. Sabra, Timothy, and the babe await me. Mother, will you go with me?"

He saw the poignant longing in his son's eyes. He gruffly said, "Go with him, Michal, as Miriam and her family surely will do. Ara can leave Zerah for me. I feel I must tarry."

★★★

Benjamin watched the caravan out of sight a short time later, wondering if he were a fool for not going with them. The feeling grew during the solemn Sabbath that followed. On the first day of the week, he determined to leave the next day. He arose early and strode into the city, not quite knowing why. A great furor in the marketplace greeted him. "What does this mean?" he asked an excited-looking man.

"Have you not heard? Joseph of Arimathaea and Nicodemus took Jesus down from the cross and put His body in a cave of stones." The man stopped for breath. "They rolled a great rock into the entrance of the sepulcher."

Another burst into the conversation. "The chief priests went to Pilate with a preposterous tale that this Jesus meant to rise again after three days." He laughed scornfully.

Not to be outdone, the first speaker continued the story. "The priests feared Jesus' disciples, cowards though they are, might attempt to steal the body and claim the carpenter had conquered death." He sneered. "Pilate ordered guards to stand by." He paused and licked his lips before furtively looking both ways. His voice dropped to a hoarse mutter.

"The stone is gone. The boulder it took strong men to roll into place." He gripped Benjamin's arm until his talon-like nails dug through the shepherd's sleeve and into his flesh. "The tomb is empty, save for the winding sheets used on the dead!"

Benjamin felt sweat ooze from every pore. "Where is this tomb?"

"In a garden." The man pointed.

With a mighty pull, Benjamin tore himself free. He ignored his years and ran like one pursued, never stopping until he reached the stone cave. An agitated crowd stood near. "Is it true?" Benjamin cried.

"He is not here. He is risen!" a woman cried, burying her face in her shawl.

"Woman, you are mad," a male voice accused. "His body was stolen." The argument rose to shrill heat, some claiming Jesus had actually been seen.

"Mary Magdalene, Mary the mother of James, and Salome brought sweet spices to anoint Him this very morning, for the Sabbath was past. They found the stone rolled away." The speaker's voice rattled in her throat. "They entered. A young man in a long, white garment sat on the right side. He knew they sought Jesus of

Nazareth. He said —" Her voice rose higher and glory filled her face. "He said Jesus was risen. They were to go their way and tell His disciples and Peter that He had gone to Galilee and they would see Him there."

Bit by bit, Benjamin separated the truth from the chaff of information sweeping the city. He found and talked with those who said they had seen Jesus face to face. Mary of Magdala. Cleopas and a kinsman who walked the dusty road from Jerusalem to Emmaus accompanied by One they knew not. Their eyes were opened when He broke bread, blessed it, and gave it to them.

Not long after, Ara returned from Bethlehem with Timothy. Miriam's gold pieces would provide food and lodging for them and Zerah. "Pray that Jesus comes before we are forced to go back to Bethlehem," Benjamin told the others.

"He will," Timothy confidently said. "When He comes, I shall run to you and we will go to Him." He grinned. "I wonder if He will remember you, Father?"

"I feel Jesus knows more about me, nay, more about all of us than we ourselves know," Ara soberly told him.

★★★

Timothy kept his promise on a day to live in memory. He rushed into their simple cottage and shouted, "A great crowd is gathering. There must be five hundred persons, whispering and pointing. Who can it be but Jesus?"

They hastened to the spot. Benjamin felt overwhelmed. When he stood before Jesus, what should he do? He noticed those around him stood with downcast faces. Did they feel the same? The need to explain how long one had searched or how hard it had been turned to vapor in the reality of His Presence.

Ara pushed through the crowd and made a way for Benjamin. Timothy perched on Ara's shoulder, as he once rode on his grandfather's. "There He is!"

His treble call sent a burst of thankfulness through Benjamin. Ara stepped back and allowed his father to move in front of him. The old shepherd fastened his gaze on Jesus' face. He felt on the verge of a great discovery, one that eluded him in the urgency of the moment.

Was Jesus the one who visited Benjamin in his dream long ago? Yea, for although he had not seen Jesus' face, the same spirit Benjamin had felt then flowed through him.

One look into His face, a single glance at the scars in His upraised hands, answered each unspoken question, fulfilled every prophecy.

A great sense of unworthiness swept over the belated follower. He knelt before the nail-scarred feet visible below Jesus' robe. Ara and Timothy knelt beside him. When they dared look up again, Jesus had gone.

Timothy stared into his grandfather's face. "You look young again, as young as my father, were it not for your white hair."

"You must never forget," Benjamin told him. He raised his hands in blessing. "You must tell it in story and song to those who come after I am gone. Timothy, whose name means to honor God, you shall be a witness of the truth all the days of your life." The look in the lad's clear eyes showed he understood. "On the morrow, we return to Bethlehem. Michal, Sabra, and the others will eagerly await our coming. Praise to Jehovah, what news we have for them!"

Some time later word came from Jerusalem. Jesus tarried with His apostles for a time, teaching them to watch, pray, and tell others about Him. He promised to return, then disappeared from Mt. Olivet. Those present testified that even while they looked steadfastly toward heaven as Jesus went up, two men in white apparel stood by them.

They said, "Ye men of Galilee, why stand ye gazing up into heaven? This same Jesus, which is taken up from you into heaven, shall so come in like manner as ye have seen Him go into heaven."

"How could Jesus go to heaven in a cloud?" Sara's face puckered.

"Jesus can do anything, my sister." Timothy crossed his arms over his wiry body. "You would know, if you had seen Him, as I did."

"Will I ever see Jesus?" Sara wistfully said.

"Someday." Not a shred of doubt marred Timothy's reply. It brought back the happy smile Sara usually wore.

Now joy and peace rested on the smiling land. Benjamin and Michal's love shone brighter than the star that once led wise men to Bethlehem. So did Sabra and Ara's devotion. Changing seasons brought other babes, brothers and sisters Timothy guarded and loved. If a special place lay in his heart for little Ara, due to the circumstances of his coming, Timothy kept his own counsel.

"If I could live all the days of my life here with you, and be a man like you, Jehovah would be pleased," he told Benjamin.

Keen of mind but bent from the passing years, Benjamin bowed his head. What had he done to be so revered? "Nay, lad. Be a man like your father."

"I shall." Timothy grinned and looked more like a boy than a young man. "He is very like you."

When he brought home a devout wife whose expressive eyes showed how much she loved Timothy, Benjamin whispered to Michal, "Can they ever know the happiness we have shared? You are lovely as the day I first beheld you."

She smiled in her gentle way. "You are growing blind, beloved, not to see my white hair. Yea, they will be happy. They have each other — and God. See?" She pointed toward Ara and Sabra, laughing together, hands joined. "They have also found the secret of life. Each gives to the other and finds strength and joy."

When the merriment ended and Michal lay sleeping, Benjamin slipped outside. He knelt on a knoll above the quiet sheep. "My cup overflows," he said. "Yet my heart is troubled. I am an old man. Before I see Jesus again, I must know. Can a belated follower be fully forgiven? Can I be as acceptable as those who turned from the sheep in the field and left all to follow Thee?"

The low words sounded loud in his ears. Not even Michal knew the shame Benjamin had carried from the moment he peered into the empty manger at Bethlehem. Neither had he confessed it to his God — until now.

The stars took on new luster. The night wind stilled until silence itself rang in Benjamin's ears. No shimmering radiance came. Instead, the same tingling he had felt kneeling at Jesus' feet after He had risen spread throughout the old man's body. Guilt fell like a bundle of sticks from a small boy's weary arms.

"It does not matter." Benjamin straightened his bent shoulders. "A man may search for thirty-three years or a hundred and thirty-three. It is of little importance, so long as he finds the Promised One at the end of his journey."

Benjamin stared at the night sky. Jesus had spoken of a kingdom not of this world, one ruled by Jehovah and His Son, where all who believed in Him would one day live forever. His pulse quickened. Had not the white-clad messengers asked the men of Galilee, "Why stand ye gazing up into heaven? This same Jesus, which is taken up from you . . . shall so come in like manner. . ."

Perhaps Jesus would return on a starry night like this, or when dawn softly colored the eastern sky, Benjamin mused. It might be in the midst of a fiery sunset, a sweeping storm, or shadowy blue dusk. It mattered not. From this moment, the belated follower would walk with his Master, no longer behind.

The employees of Thorndike Press hope you have enjoyed this Large Print book. All our Large Print titles are designed for easy reading, and all our books are made to last. Other Thorndike Press Large Print books are available at your library, through selected bookstores, or directly from us.

For information about titles, please call:

(800) 223-1244

To share your comments, please write:

Publisher
Thorndike Press
P.O. Box 159
Thorndike, Maine 04986